Christin
Armstrong

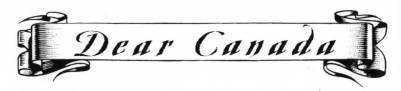

Alone in an Untamed Land

The *Filles du Roi* Diary of Hélène St. Onge

BY MAXINE TROTTIER

Scholastic Canada Ltd.

SALSO

Reignac, France,
1666

le 8 mai 1666

This was not always my diary. I found it in the library as I searched for a book one day. Was it Maman's or Papa's? Both sets of their initials are written on the first page, all entwined. Sadly, I will never know which of them gave it to the other. I have claimed it as my own, and have written my name upon its cover: Hélène St. Onge.

I cannot remember Maman, since I was an infant when she died, but Papa, dear Papa, I shall never forget. He is gone now as well, smallpox having taken him this winter, although in my heart I am certain that at least in part he died of sadness and loss. Writing in this journal will be a little like talking to him, I think. How I miss talking to him.

There is Catherine, of course. I love my sister very much, but she is sixteen years of age and I am thirteen. Catherine is quite grand. I am not. Sometimes it seems as if fifty years separate us rather than three.

le 9 mai 1666

There is so much to write, if I am to keep this as a proper record of my life. Where to begin, though? I might write all about myself, although I am not very interesting. I am plain, with green eyes and a pointed chin. Catherine says I look like my cat Minette. She does not say this to be cruel. It is only the truth. *Meow*, I say back to her. I may have large eyes, but I certainly do not have black fur.

Papa once told me that the morning I was born a fierce storm arose, and I came into this world in the midst of it. A lovely rainbow spread itself across the sky and Papa held me up so that my first sight of the world might be one of beauty. I smiled. My old nurse, Louise, says it would only have been gas, but Papa always insisted that it was a smile. Rainbows still make me smile.

le 10 mai 1666

Today I thought I had lost Minette. She does love to wander. Our home has twenty rooms after all, and many excellent places to hide. There is also the barn or the stable if you do not mind the smell of manure, and I do not. Sometimes, like Minette, I roam in the meadows and woods, or climb the thick branches of the old oak trees. Catherine would not approve of the climbing.

I found Minette at last in the library, which, after my chamber, is my favourite place in this house. It was Papa's favourite room also. How many hours had he spent here working on his book, writing in his journal, carrying on the work he was never to finish? I keep that journal with my own things now. *A Treatise on the Natures of Men and Dragonflies*, it was to be called. I have copied one of his drawings of a dragonfly onto the first page of this diary in his memory.

Except for the rooms we use, the house is rather dusty, since there are no servants here now. The library, though, is clean. I myself see to that. Its tables and shelves are polished, the floor gleams, and the books are in order. There is no odour of mustiness, for I open the windows every week and let the fresh air blow in. I sometimes sit alone here in the evening with a single candle and write in this diary, as I am now doing. Louise says I must not waste candles.

Once I opened a book to find that an iris had been pressed between its pages. Had Maman put it there? Again, I will not ever know. That is why it is so important for me to write in this diary. Some day I may have a daughter. If I am not here, the words I write will tell my story.

le 14 mai 1666

It rained yesterday and today. Minette does not care for the rain and so she stayed inside, lazy creature. She watched the rain run down the glass of the window in the library and put out her paw to bat at it. Does she think it is alive? I asked her, but all she did was meow. That is silly, I know, but what luxury it is to be silly, even if it is only in writing. All that will end when I grow older and marry, Louise says.

Marriage. What a serious thing. It is very likely that Catherine will wed a young man by the name of Armand Lecôté. He lives with his family in Montréal, across the ocean in New France, and his father is an old acquaintance of Papa's. It took many letters and much bargaining to arrange such a thing. Catherine, fortunately, has a fine dowry and anyone would wed her.

Catherine says I must put childish things aside and act like the young lady I am.

Perhaps I should, but I would rather take off my shoes and stockings and run through the puddles in the garden.

le 17 mai 1666

Letters arrived while I was out walking with Minette in the garden. One was all the way from New France. Catherine read it, of course. Monsieur Lecôté has expressed his regrets at the death of Papa. He wished to know the state of Catherine's dowry.

Strangely, there was no letter from Armand, but there was a letter from Cousin Pierre Demerse in La Rochelle. Cousin Pierre and his wife, Cousine Madeleine, will come here to live. Catherine says it is because Cousin Pierre is our guardian, and Papa's will was quite clear that he should look out for us until we wed. They will bring their daughter, Cousine Anne.

le 18 mai 1666

Cousin Pierre, Cousine Madeleine and Cousine Anne arrived in a large coach this morning. Three housemaids, a cook and a rather haughty butler rode behind them in a little cart.

Servants! Now the house will be sparkling clean again.

le 19 mai 1666

It rained all day today. Cousin Pierre shut himself up in Papa's study and did not come out until the afternoon. When he did, his face was grim. They did not see me, for I was hiding behind the screen in the hall, but Cousin Pierre told Madeleine that the debts are great, so great the house must be sold.

"Insects! Dragonflies! All his life the fool wasted

time and money in his pointless work. Now it has come to this!" he fumed. Then he sighed. "I had suspected as much. I thank *le bon Dieu* that I wrote to Monsieur Deschamps before we set out. The girls are my responsibility, and I will see them safely settled somehow."

I cannot sleep. One by one, each thing in my life that meant anything to me has been taken away. Maman, Papa, and now my home will be gone. I will have only Catherine, and Minette of course, loyal Minette who hisses each time she sees Madeleine.

le 23 mai 1666

The days grow more miserable and the only place I may write in peace is here in my own chamber. How I miss the use of our library!

Catherine says Madeleine does not wish to have two unmarried females under this roof, especially if young men come to call. Anne is more important, since she is eighteen and of a marriageable age. More nonsense. I think that Madeleine and Anne are jealous of Catherine. My sister is so lovely.

Madeleine looks like one of the sheep that stands staring from behind a fence. Does that make Anne a lamb? She is not very lamb-like. It is not Madeleine's fault that she looks like a sheep, but she need not act like one.

le 24 mai 1666

I think Cousine Madeleine would very much like us to leave. This morning she said that there is barely enough room for us to stay here. What does she mean? *Le Cadeau* has twenty rooms! We must make ourselves useful, she says.

"I can embroider and make lace," Catherine offered. "My soufflés are very light."

I said that I could cook and do most tasks in the kitchen. Before they were sold, I often helped milk the cows. It was how I caught the cowpox, and why my hands have the little scars that they bear.

Cousine Madeleine did not seem impressed.

I do wish Armand would write.

le 25 mai 1666

Catherine and Madeleine argued today.

"There will be no dowries for you once the house is sold and the debts are paid," Madeleine said. "Armand Lecôté will never marry you now."

I myself do not believe that Madeleine is correct. Armand loves Catherine. He said so once in a letter that made me laugh, he tried so hard to be flowery and romantic.

"Enough, Madeleine," Cousin Pierre said, stepping between Catherine and his wife. "I have made inquires at the convent, Catherine," he said to her gently. "You would be welcome there as a novice. Hélène, as well, in time. It could be a good life for you both. I would, naturally, provide modest dowries."

Catherine wept bitterly tonight. It is Madeleine's fault. I am too cross to weep. A pair of nuns, indeed!

le 26 mai 1666

I have sinned. I called Madeleine a sheep. I was sent directly to my chamber without dinner. I will admit that Papa sent me up more than once when I was naughty, but never did he starve me. How fortunate that I keep bread and cheese in a tin inside the armoire in case Minette or I require food during the night.

This morning I walked to Père Simard to make my confession. I am ashamed to say I enjoyed the walk from our house to the church in our village of Reignac. He made very strange choking noises on the other side of the little screen when I told him what I had said. I hope he does not take ill. My penance is to pray the rosary every night for a week. I have added to the penance myself. I will apologize to Madeleine.

Before I left the confessional, I asked Père Simard if keeping the diary might be a sin of pride. He said no. I do tend to be a little proud of how well I write.

Catherine's letters are blotched and misspelled. I suspect that Madeleine and Anne can barely write or read at all.

Papa always said that there is enormous power in the written word and that I must use it for good things. I know in my heart that this diary is a good thing, but it is always best to ask a priest.

le 28 mai 1666

Today visitors came. I crouched down in the hallway, my ear next to the partially opened door, and listened.

He was Monsieur Deschamps, the man to whom Cousin Pierre had written. She was Madame Laurent. Both of them are from Montréal. Do they know Armand?

"You have royal blood, Mademoiselle St. Onge, and you would be a highly desirable bride for someone of the upper class," Madame Laurent said to Catherine.

It is true we are related to His Majesty Louis XIV. A few drops of royal blood course through our veins, we have always been told. But we are so distantly related that Louise says it does not matter. Still, it is not something that everyone may claim.

They then proposed something to Catherine that took the very breath from my lungs.

"Would you consider leaving France to become one of *les filles à marier*?" Monsieur Deschamps asked her. "It would not be such a hardship, since you have family in Montréal, Monsieur Demerse tells me."

This was true. Papa's brother Jules, who died years ago, lived in Montréal and married a widow. No one except Papa ever spoke of her. There had been letters when Oncle Jules was alive, but they slowly ended, the way things sometimes do. Her name is Barbe Moitié.

"The woman keeps a tavern, monsieur," snapped Catherine. Then she asked, "What is this you are proposing? Who are *les filles à marier*?"

Before I could hear the answer, Louise caught me on my knees and sent me away.

"Manners, Hélène. Manners," she scolded.

I may perish of curiosity. Is excessive curiosity a sin? I must ask Père Simard at confession. I will walk to the church this instant, just in case it is.

ce même soir

I may now finish this entry, since Père Simard has explained. There are not enough women in New France. No men are marrying, and so no babies are being born. The officials in New France put great pressure upon single men, even forbidding them to

12

leave the towns or trade with the Indians unless they wed.

Les filles à marier. Père Simard said that they are the girls chosen by the merchants of the *Compagnie des Indes Occidentales* and sometimes the priests. The girls are carefully screened, and only the best are chosen. He will be writing a letter of recommendation for Catherine if she goes. She will need her birth certificate as well.

They receive a dowry in the form of a little chest of goods. Their duty is to wed and to raise children, all for the glory of God and the King. In Montréal, they stay with a woman named la Soeur Marguerite Bourgeoys who looks after them. La Soeur Bourgeoys is a nun and could not be more respectable. If they receive an offer of marriage, they themselves decide whether they will marry that man. Then when they marry, there is a gift of money, or a cow or some chickens.

New France sounds so exciting and mysterious. The thought of travelling so far from all I have ever known does worry me a little, though, I admit. But there is Tante Barbe, after all. Catherine thinks she cannot possibly be respectable. Papa did not agree. A woman must live, he always said, and a tavern can be a decent place. I know nothing of such things, but if Papa said so, it is the truth.

Could anything be more splendid for Catherine

than to become a *fille à marier*? I am not so certain the cow is splendid, though.

le 3 juin 1666

Catherine and I have talked and talked. She does not normally ask my opinion, but there is no one to ask but me anymore, and hers is a hard choice to make. What Monsieur Deschamps proposed could be the means to our salvation. The King will provide a dowry, just as though Catherine were his own daughter. She will be under His Majesty's protection. I will be too, for Catherine will not agree to this unless I am permitted to come along. I had a grand idea. I will be her housekeeper when she is married and we will be together.

le 5 juin 1666

Monsieur Deschamps returned today. An agreement has been reached. I may accompany her, but since I am so young Catherine insisted it will not be as a *fille à marier*, even though some girls even younger than I have married there. I cannot imagine marrying at eleven or twelve years of age.

Monsieur Deschamps seemed to think it would be perfectly correct. "Come now, mademoiselle," he said. "Would you not like to be the wife of a Montréal merchant?"

I could not help myself. I burst out that I was but thirteen years old.

"Ridiculous," Catherine said to Monsieur Deschamps. "My sister will not marry until she is a woman. And she will not wed some stranger she meets in a faraway town in New France who only wishes to have anyone for his wife. It will be someone she knows and respects, as I will marry Armand. This dowry will be sufficient in his eyes, monsieur."

Monsieur Deschamps and Cousin Pierre looked at each other in a way I disliked. They said nothing. I can only pray that Catherine knows Armand as well as she believes that she does.

le 6 juin 1666

We leave on Friday. The mass this Sunday morning was the last I shall ever attend at our church in Reignac. I prayed that both Catherine and I will have the strength to make the journey and leave our dear home behind.

Monsieur Deschamps has travelled on ahead to the ship, but Madame Laurent has remained here at *Le Cadeau* so that she might act as our chaperone on the journey. She is a pleasant woman, pink-cheeked and jolly, and I think it will be a pleasure to travel with her.

It will be a journey of three days or so from here. We are to go by Cousin Pierre's coach to La Rochelle and then sail to New France. There will not be room for us to take much, only a few chests. Mine will be the small one, since Catherine has so many lovely things as a bride.

Cousin Pierre has shown us a kindness in the form of a gift of money. Fifty *livre*s. It is generous, I suppose, and I pray it will be enough. As a *fille à marier* Catherine has one hundred *livres*. Some of that is for clothing, and sixty for the ship's passage. Monsieur Deschamps received ten *livres* from that as a fee for enlisting her. I understand his eagerness now.

Madame Laurent says that it may be possible to procure more private accommodations on the ship. Those with no money must share a common space. Catherine wrinkles her nose to think of such a thing, but it could be most interesting.

le 7 juin 1666

I have helped Louise carefully fold and pack Catherine's trousseau. Cousine Madeleine and Anne watched us. Madeleine made a suggestion once or twice. She does know a good deal about the care of fine clothing, as she has so much of it herself. We tucked in small bags of herbs among the garments, for the lavender, peppermint, cloves and thyme will keep the cloth sweet smelling. There is another chest with our bedding, sheets and quilts and such. It has worn me out, and so I am writing this in bed.

I packed my own things alone in my room. Stockings, shifts, pockets, aprons, handkerchiefs, shoes, caps, a *coiffe*, a comb, a warm shawl, an everyday gown with its skirt and bodice, and a gown for church. Cleaning sticks for my teeth, my rosary and my prayer book. Some small skeins of brightly coloured linen thread, and my *lucet* for making cord. It is all crammed into my chest.

I bent down to pick up a ribbon that had dropped onto the carpet, and when I turned to my chest, there was Minette sitting inside it. It brought tears to my eyes. I picked her up and she purred in contentment.

"No, Minette," I said sadly. "You cannot come." I told her that she must stay here with Louise or go to the barn. She must be a good, brave cat and keep away all the mice. I had decided that I will take her collar and leash with me, as a memento, but she must stay home. Catherine said it was very silly of me to bring along something so unnecessary.

Life is unfair.

le 10 juin 1666

I think that I have never been more happy and sad and fearful all at the same time. There will be no sleep for me this night, I fear, for tomorrow we are to begin the grand adventure. I may as well write.

Here I lie, all wrapped in feather quilts. How odd it will be, after tonight, not to sleep in the same bed in which I have slept since I left the nursery.

The bed curtains have not yet been let down, and one candle burns on the small table next to me. It is the last time I will spend a night here, and I must set down every detail so that when I am old I will recall it clearly.

As always, Louise scolded that I should not drip ink upon the coverlet, and asked if I had said my prayers. I can be forgetful. But there was no anger in her voice, for she already missed us. She is worried about us too, though she tries not to show it.

I put down my quill and hugged her. I assured her that I would take care, that my prayers had been said, and see how well I had braided my hair. I must do it for myself now and I must dress Catherine's hair just as Louise has shown me. It would not do for a *fille à marier* to appear untidy.

At this, she sniffed and gave a sad sigh. "*Bien*," she said in approval. She told me to put out my candle and go to sleep. The journey to the ship and La

Rochelle tomorrow would begin early. I begged for more time, knowing she would not refuse me.

Picking up her own candle, she shook her head hopelessly, kissed my forehead and bid me sleep well. At the door she asked, "You do not have Minette in bed with you again, do you? She sheds black hair over everything."

I told her that of course I did not have Minette in bed, speaking as innocently as I could. Minette began her low, steady purring at the sound of my voice saying her name. Louise did not hear her though, and even if she did, I knew she would say nothing this last night.

When Louise closed the door, Minette crawled out, shook herself and scattered black hairs upon the coverlet. She began to wash, first one paw, then the other and then her face.

Ah, Minette, I said to myself, stroking her back. She arched up, warm and soft under my hand. I picked her up and hugged her, and she purred very loudly. Tears came to my eyes, although I loathe to cry.

le 11 juin 1666

Catherine is asleep next to me here in our room at the inn, where we have stopped for the night. I myself am exhausted, but far too excited to sleep.

Besides, I fear that if I do not record the day's events, I may forget them by morning.

This morning I dressed myself by candlelight. First, a fresh linen shift, then warm stockings with buckled garters. Heavy shoes would keep my feet dry if it was damp. Then the hated *corps*. It is no easy task to put on a *corps* unassisted, and, although I did not lace myself in as tightly as Louise always did, it would suffice. Minette made it more difficult than usual, since she wound around my legs the entire time.

I put on a bodice and skirt of plain grey wool. The gown suits me. I do not care so much for fashion, and if I am warm and dry, nothing else matters. I would wear little jewellery. I had at my neck the cross that Papa made for Maman before they were wed, and on my finger, the silver mourning ring I have worn since Papa died. The mirror showed me a thin girl with a serious expression. I made a horrible face at this girl as I combed and put up my hair.

I picked up the candle and walked down the hallway to Catherine's chamber to help her ready herself for the journey. Minette followed me as far as the door, and then scampered off in search of her breakfast in the kitchen.

There was Catherine in her shift, her long blond hair hanging down her back. To me she was as lovely as a princess. We do not look the least alike, for she is fair and I am dark. Her eyes are a clear blue, but this morning they were red, and I know she had been weeping, as I had.

She smiled bravely. "Come lace me into my *corps*, Hélène." She would wear the yellow travelling gown today.

I asked if she was certain about this journey as I pulled the laces tightly to make her waist slender. I myself wonder if it is the right thing.

"There is nothing for me here, Hélène. I could have entered the convent and become a holy sister. It is a good life, but not one I wish to live. My path will be far different as a *fille à marier*," she said, just as I knew she would.

I helped her on with her gown. The bodice and skirt were both of fine, heavy wool. She must look a lady every moment if she is to please Armand. I braided her hair and fastened it upon her head with long pins of tortoiseshell, letting little curls dangle here and there so that her amber earrings showed between.

Before we left her chamber Catherine set her hands upon my shoulders and said, "We will be happy in New France, Hélène. I promise it."

I smiled, but did not answer. Catherine picked up her cloak and went down the stairs.

I returned to my chamber one last time. I will never see it again, I thought. For a moment, I feared that my heart would break. I closed my eyes, said a prayer for bravery and swirled my cloak over my shoulders. I had a travelling bag of embroidered fabric that once had been Maman's. In it I put my quills, this diary in which I write, a small stoppered bottle, and packets of ink powder. I had also taken Papa's journal. It would be like taking part of him with me. Clutching the bag, I went down to the entrance hall and out into the morning.

Our coach waited on the cobbles with Madame Laurent inside. The horses stamped and blew and one rolled his big brown eye back at me as if to say, "Get in, girl. I want to run!"

Louise, wrapped in her shawl, kissed us one last time before we climbed into the carriage. The few of our old servants who had come by to see us off wept and sniffled. Cousin Pierre was there, but Cousine Madeleine and Anne were still in bed. They needed their sleep, he said.

The coachman helped Catherine in first, and then me. He climbed up onto his seat. There was a snap of the coachman's whip, a jingle of harness, and the carriage began to move. Down the lane and out into the countryside it rolled. Home, Louise and Minette were becoming smaller and smaller.

Minette, I thought to myself in misery. "I did not kiss Minette farewell, Catherine," I said aloud.

At the sound of my voice Minette began to purr!

She crawled out from under the seat where she had been hiding, leaped onto my lap and rubbed against my face.

"Minette!" I cried in a rather different tone. "Oh my fine Minette! You are coming with us after all." I dug in my bag, pulled out her collar and buckled it on.

"We cannot take a cat to New France," said Madame Laurent. I will never forget the exasperation in her voice. She lifted her hand to rap on the roof and signal the coachman to stop.

I protested that if we were going, why might not a cat?

I thought I knew my sister Catherine very, very well. She opened her mouth to argue, to say some thing about dignity or appearances, but then she closed her lips and patted my hand.

"Why not indeed, Hélène? If we are going, why should Minette not come along? There are mice and rats in New France, are there not, madame? Surely a cat such as she will find her place there."

Madame Laurent only shrugged.

"We are going to New France, Minette," I murmured into her thick coat. And I thought to myself that now I was certain that I would not mind it so very much.

le 12 juin 1666

We were all tired when we stopped at this inn for the night, and I fell asleep quickly. But I have had a dream that woke me, and so I lit a candle and will write a while.

I had dreamed of home, of a place I will never see again. I will not watch the lambs play in the fields near Reignac. They will grow to be fat sheep, their wool will be woven into shawls and blankets, and I will never see any of it, for I will be far away when that happens. Pears will ripen in the orchard all through the summer, the harvest will be brought home, the roof of our old house will be covered in snow, and then frogs will begin to peep in the woods beyond the meadow in spring.

There will be another home for us some day.

I will put out the candle now. Perhaps I will dream of that new home.

le 13 juin 1666

La Rochelle is remarkable. I am used to odours; the dovecote was all feathery and the barn had milk cows and sometimes their calves. The sheepfold had its own smell of wool. But this! There are horse droppings, fresh fish and whatever flows in the gutters all mingling together. The inn at which we stopped at a late hour is smoky and smells of people.

Fortunately, there are good smells as well. The innkeeper's wife had a pot of mussel soup with cream, which we had for our dinner. There was fresh bread. When we went to the room Catherine and I were to share, it was stuffy and warm. I threw open the window and there was the smell of the sea. The small room, which Catherine judged to be far beneath us, is at least clean. Madame Laurent has her own chamber, but Catherine and I share a bed. I myself do not mind this at all, especially since Minette is here to purr me to sleep.

Tomorrow the last part of our journey will begin.

le 14 juin 1666

We arrived at the ship this evening. She is charmingly called *Le Chat Blanc*. Captain Renville greeted us. He is a loud, red-faced man. We went deep inside the ship to where a single lantern hung from the ceiling. Monsieur Deschamps was seated there at a table that also hung from the ceiling by ropes.

The captain gave Catherine the lantern he carried and said, "Mesdemoiselles, if you are to have a candle, it must be within a lantern. Fire is a fearsome danger aboard a ship. We do not wish to fry in our beds. *Bon soir*." With that cheerful thought, he left us.

"You have this small cabin," said Madame Laurent, leading us back. "Monsieur Deschamps has that one. I myself will be quartered with the girls in the Sainte-Barbe, as is proper."

I cannot imagine how we will manage together in this small room for all the weeks to come. Still, we were fortunate to acquire even such a small place to ourselves. It is better than what the other girls face. They must share beds, and all they have for privacy is a curtain. And their beds are among the cannons! That is why the room is called the Sainte-Barbe, I learned. She is the patron saint of cannoniers.

Sailors brought down our chests. Our clothing and few possessions we may keep with us, but our bedding chest we emptied. It is to be stored in the bottom of the ship with barrels and such. We made our bed, Catherine and I. Or rather, I made it and she pulled the sheets and quilts every which way. We will be crowded here. The ceiling is low, the chests are in the way and the bed, or the berth as they call it, is narrow. I cannot wait for tomorrow to come so that I might explore the ship and meet the other *filles à marier*.

There is one tiny cabin not yet occupied. I wonder who will have it?

le 15 juin 1666

I woke this morning before dawn to the most peculiar world. I have been in a boat before. There was a small punt Papa used to keep at the pond and I fell out of it many times. Thank goodness that pond was shallow. But I have not ever seen anything like this ship that will take us across the ocean. It is like being inside some sea creature all made of wood. It groans and creaks all around me. Minette does not care for that at all, but like me, she will have to become comfortable with it.

We dressed one at a time since the cabin is so cramped. Catherine normally would have grumbled, but she is so unhappy with this that she said nothing, only stood there with tears in her eyes.

I tried to make her laugh, saying that the cabin was a mere closet, but it was *our* closet. She did not laugh.

Out in the common room, we had eggs and bread for breakfast. There were pears and slices of lemon. I shared my eggs with Minette.

"Eat the fruit," Madame Laurent insisted. "There is fresh food now, but once we have been at sea for a while, all we will get is salt eels or salt pork."

Later there were bells, bells, bells. They ring to mark the half hours on each watch. Perhaps I will become accustomed to them.

I shall explore.

le 17 juin 1666

I am not a *fille à marier*, and so not really under the guardianship of Monsieur Deschamps or Madame Laurent, but rather of Catherine. Madame and Monsieur feel I am their responsibility nonetheless, and do not like that I go out on the deck by myself. What am I to do? Catherine has a headache and I believe it is best she is left alone in the quiet to rest.

Not that there will be much quiet, for *les filles à marier* have begun to come aboard. They are of all sizes and shapes, some as young as I am, but most at least as old as Catherine, it appears. They laugh and tease each other and make jokes about the husbands they will wed. How friendly they all are.

I will set their names down here so that I do not forget. There are eight girls from the *Salpêtrière*. That is the girls' orphanage in Paris. They are Bernice, Jeanne, Eloise, Marguerite, Celine, Cecile, Claudette and Lise. They do not look overly healthy to me. There are also five girls all named Marie. They are country girls, strong, hardy and quite merry.

I shall never sort out the Maries, since I am hopeless with names. It is easier to remember who they are by how they look. For this diary, they will be Marie with the mole beside her mouth, Marie with the freckles, short Marie, Marie who never speaks, and Marie with the missing front tooth. I really think they would not mind.

le 18 juin 1666

Captain Renville, for all his loudness and his red face, is a kind man. He showed the girls and me the ship today. Catherine did not care to see it.

His cabin is at the back of the vessel, which they call the stern. It stretches all across and has large windows. You can look out whenever you wish and see where the ship has sailed by the white wake it leaves in the water. At least Captain Renville may, for he shares this room with no one. He has many books there. I wanted to ask if I might borrow one. Perhaps another day. How my fingers ached to turn the pages.

The cabin in which Catherine and I reside is ahead of the captain's. The common sailors and any male passengers sleep all together in one room that is near the front of the ship. There is a kitchen, or a galley, and even a manger for the chickens, pigs and goats. I would like to think that these animals will see New France, but I have been told that they will not. They will be eaten.

le 19 juin 1666

Catherine is most unhappy with our companions. They are coarse girls, she says, country bumpkins and slatterns, and I must not associate with them. This I ignore. They may be our neighbours in time.

Marie with the missing front tooth proudly showed me the small chest provided for each of the girls by the King. Catherine had declined her chest.

"I have never had so many nice things," Marie exclaimed. "None of us have. Look at this, Hélène. Stockings, gloves, ribbon and shoelaces, needles, a comb. Such a lovely handkerchief. See, there is more. Then when we marry we will receive perhaps thirty *livres*. Think of it!"

I thought of all Catherine's costly possessions. It made me feel odd.

le 20 juin 1666

A priest came aboard the ship this morning and we had our first mass. He is Père Denis, a Jesuit, and Madame Laurent says he is returning to New France to the missions there. Père Denis is tall and rather unkempt. He is nearly bald except for a fringe of red hair that goes round his head.

Père Denis brought all the girls together for prayers this evening. Madame and Monsieur were there, naturally. Monsieur Deschamps looked very important in his full breeches and coat, his moustache and chin tuft neatly combed. On his head, atop his wig, perched an elegant beaver hat. This he took off and set carefully down on a chair. The hat, not the wig.

Père Denis began leading us in the rosary. I thought that perhaps he cast an interested eye upon that hat once or twice. I am certain it was my imagination. It would keep his bald head warm, though, in the winters of New France. Perhaps he should purchase a wig.

Since then I have thought about that hat of Monsieur Deschamps. It is made of felted beaver hair. They say there are many beavers in New France. Monsieur Deschamps says that a man must have a licence to trade for the furs and, to keep that licence, these days a man must marry. I am not certain if I feel more sorry for the girls or the men. I am grateful to *le bon Dieu* that I am not in such a position.

le 21 juin 1666

It is night. I am safe and warm in the bed here next to Catherine, but I cannot help wondering what lies ahead. We will sail before dawn, to catch the outgoing tide. Other people came onto the ship during the day, all bound for New France. I intend to speak with each one of them, if I can. There are merchants, and farmers, and even a young girl that they say is an Indian. I have not met an Indian before, and so I must certainly introduce myself to her. She is the answer to the mystery of the empty cabin. It is to be hers.

I wonder about New France. Will I see beavers there? The country is wild and beautiful, they have told us, and dangerous beyond belief. Papa used to say that knowledge gives strength. If I am to have the strength to leave all I have ever known and help Catherine in her marriage, then I believe I must learn all I can.

le 22 juin 1666

I stood on deck and watched France disappear in the mist. Catherine stayed inside the ship, *below*, the captain calls it. But I had to watch. I may never see France again.

I wept. My cheeks were damp with the mist and so I think that no one saw. I did not care if they did. I only wished to be alone inside myself and let the image of France burn into my mind. Then I heard a sound. It was the Indian girl. She had come up on deck and now stood at the ship's rail near me. Her cheeks were as wet with tears as mine were. There was a difference, I soon learned from her. My tears were of loss, born from the idea of leaving France. Hers were tears of joy.

"I am going home," she said.

Her words sounded strange to me. She spoke French, but with an accent I have never heard.

le 23 juin 1666

Her name is Kateri Aubry. She is half French and half Mohawk. Her father, Monsieur Jean Aubry, is a gunsmith who keeps a shop in Montréal. He must do well to be able to afford the cabin for her alone. He himself has a place forward with the sailors.

Kateri's mother died two years before in childbirth. The baby had been a girl. How strange that we have both lost our mamans. Kateri is luckier than I am though, for she has her papa to love. Like me she has a dear pet, a dog named Ourson, since she says he looks like a little bear. It was necessary to leave him with a neighbour. She looks forward to seeing him again.

She is interesting, this Kateri. She is ten years of age, and she is different from anyone I have ever seen. Her skin is a rosy brown colour and her cheekbones slant up charmingly. She has thick black hair that hangs perfectly straight, although she wears it in a long braid. Her eyes are dark, and she has her father's smile. She has told me this, and so I have to take it as the truth. Monsieur Aubry is a silent, unsmiling man who seldom looks at anyone. He is pleasant in his appearance, some might say very pleasant, with light brown hair and brown eyes.

She and her father are returning to Montréal

after a visit to his family in France. He misses his wife, I think. He has the same look about him that Papa sometimes had.

Catherine cannot understand why I would want to spend time with Kateri. "We shall make our friends among the better people in Montréal," she says.

If I avoided everyone whom Catherine thought was below our station or of little interest, I would be lonely indeed. Besides, Minette likes Kateri and she is the best judge of character that I know. Minette even likes the serious Monsieur Aubry. She rubs against his legs, but he ignores her.

I think Kateri and I shall be friends in time.

le 24 juin 1666

Today is the feast of Corpus Christi. Madame Laurent invited Kateri to join us for mass and she did, since she is most devout. Monsieur Aubry is not devout, it appears. He remained on the exact opposite side of the ship, on the left when facing toward the front of the ship. The larboard, as Captain Renville calls it. The other side where we knelt to pray is the starboard. Would not left and right be simpler?

le 26 juin 1666

I have met a ship's boy named Séraphin Poule. He looks quite strong and much older than his fifteen years. He wears his long red hair in a braid and his skin is brown from the sun. Séraphin has had a hard life, I think, having been a sailor since he was just six. There is a coarseness about him, but he is quite sociable, and says he will tell me anything I want to know about the ship if he is not at some heavy task. I want to know everything.

Fortunately, Madame Laurent or Monsieur Deschamps come above only for a brief while each day to take the air. If they were on the deck, they would probably consider it inappropriate that I speak with Séraphin. Perhaps it is. I have prayed about whether or not keeping this from them is a lie. Papa always said that I must learn all I can in this life. I am not certain that Papa was referring to sailing vessels, but I have decided that he would approve.

Le Chat Blanc is not a big ship as ships go, Séraphin has told me. All ships are to be referred to as females, and so *she* is a galleon of about 17 *toise* in length. There are three masts and endless numbers of canvas sails that are put up or taken down depending on the whim of the captain. There are six cannons to protect us if we are set upon by pirates. I refuse to think of pirates.

Sailors climb to the sails on ladders of rope called *enflecheures* or ratlings. I do not want to consider how these ladders have come by their name. There are many rats down in the hold, they say. Minette will make short work of them.

Séraphin knows the names of all the sails. He rattles them off for Kateri in the same way that I could name all the flowers and herbs of our garden at home.

That was an error, to think of the garden. I miss home. Madeleine had best be taking care of that garden properly, and so had the person who buys our house.

le 28 juin 1666

I have not been able to see land for six days. Our bedding has an unpleasant dampness to it now, but I am still grateful for the privacy I have as I write this.

Séraphin said, "We will not see land again for perhaps three months, mademoiselle. I do hope you enjoy the sight of water."

I knew this, but to hear it from the mouth of a sailor made it seem too real.

The weather is fine and the wind is blowing smartly. Seabirds, I have no idea as to what sort, soar above us. Often they do not even flap their wings. How astonishing it must be to have such freedom, to journey anywhere that the wind takes you. This journey is like that for me, although I cannot tell Catherine of such ideas.

le 30 juin 1666

Catherine came out on deck today for the first time. What a stir that caused. She stood with Madame Laurent and Monsieur Deschamps in the sunshine. The other *filles à marier* were there as well, but no one had eyes for anyone except Catherine. She is so lovely. Little wisps of her blond hair blew about like gold threads escaping from the *coiffe* and the ribbons she was wearing.

Only Monsieur Aubry did not notice Catherine. How peculiar. He watched the sky and talked with Captain Renville, who was also staring upwards. They spoke quietly together and no matter how I strained my ears, I could not hear what they said. I gazed up at the sky as well. There was not a cloud against the deep blue above us, and so I can only imagine what they thought.

le 3 juillet 1666

The wind blew hard during the night and the waves grew larger and larger. I could feel how the ship rose slowly up one side and slipped down the other as I knelt to say my prayers. It was extremely hard to keep my balance.

When I climbed into bed next to Catherine she asked, "Are you afraid, Hélène?"

I had left a candle burning in the hanging lantern. There was only that faint light, and I could not see her face any better than I can see this page to write these words. Catherine was all shadows. Still, I am certain that a glint of fear was in her eyes. It was exactly like the spark I once saw in the eye of a rabbit that our cook was about to kill with a sharp blow to its little neck. How uneasy that glint in Catherine's own eyes made me feel.

I was not afraid, and neither should she be, I told her. The ship is strong, the crew is capable, and the captain very brave. Besides, Minette and I were here with her.

Catherine smiled at this. She turned on her side and I think she slept.

plus tard cette nuit

I want this diary to be an honest accounting of what happens. The thought that I had been less than honest has kept me from sleep. Awake and alone now, I do not mind admitting that I am just a little frightened.

⚜

le 5 juillet 1666

I took the air this afternoon. The sky was grey and rain fell, although where the rain ends and the spray from the huge waves begins, one cannot tell. The sea is like a big snake rolling and rolling. Monsieur Aubry was on the deck. He wore no hat on his head and his brown hair blew about wildly. His plain clothing flapped in the wind like sails of brown wool. He saw me and shouted that I must go below.

I did not feel inclined to obey him. He is not my father, nor my guardian. There was something in his voice that made me disappear quickly, anyway. I should not like to anger Monsieur Aubry.

le 6 juillet 1666

There is a storm and it is becoming difficult to write, even though I have squeezed myself into a corner of our bed. Poor Minette is close beside me. The ship creaks and groans dreadfully. All of *les filles à marier* and even Madame and Monsieur are seasick. I have not seen Kateri. She must be ill as well. Monsieur Aubry I saw once as he carried a bucket away from her cabin. I was just returning from having emptied ours. He nodded to me and I think I saw respect in his eyes.

Catherine could not stop vomiting. She has nothing left to bring up. The motion of the storm does not bother me as much as the vile smell here. Buckets of vomit and the contents of the chamber pots have spilled and run across the floor. I would vomit myself except that I must care for Catherine.

le 9 juillet 1666

I fear I will not easily be able to read this later. The writing is wretched and the movement of the ship keeps me from legibility. The ink bottle spilled and there is a black stain upon the blanket.

I could bear no more this evening, and so I followed the captain up on deck so that I might have just a little clean air. Catherine slept and so I did not feel as much guilt for leaving her. What I felt when I stepped out whipped away any guilt, so enormous was my terror.

I prayed to *le bon Dieu* to save us all. And to the Sainte Vierge, Sainte Hélène and Sainte Catherine, and every other saint whose name I could recall. The sky was black and neither the moon nor stars showed. Each time lightning shot out from the clouds, I could see the ocean. The waves were larger than ever and foam blew from them. How could we survive this, I thought? I do not want to die here.

A sailor came running and shouted that I must go below. I did, although not willingly. As frightened as

I was, it was somehow difficult to tear myself away from the sight of something so powerful.

le 12 juillet 1666

Catherine continues to be seasick, as do most of the others. It is little wonder, since the air is so foul here. Illness comes from foul air.

le 13 juillet 1666

The storm has passed and the captain ordered the hatches opened. How wonderful to smell the sweet sea breezes. I begged Catherine to take a deep breath. It would make her feel better.

She did not answer me, and only opened her eyes a little. They were sticky and crusted. I wiped her face with a damp cloth. We are not to use any of our drinking water to wash ourselves, but I save a bit of mine for this. Then I patted her shoulder, tucked the blanket up to her chin, and said a prayer to Saint Eramus for her return to health. He is the patron saint of those who suffer from seasickness. I wonder if he was ever seasick himself?

I went out again. So did short Marie, Kateri and Marie with the mole beside her mouth. All were feeling stronger. It is bold, the others said, to do such things on our own, since decent girls do not wander about unaccompanied by a chaperone. I reminded them that Madame and Monsieur were both seasick and were of no use now. Besides, Minette was there with us, and she can be very fierce when she takes it into her head that I need defending.

The sun was just setting. It was so beautiful, all red and gold on the tops of the waves. I wish Catherine could have seen it.

le 14 juillet 1666

The sailors danced on the deck this morning. One of them played a small flute and another beat upon a drum. It was a happy sound, the laughter and the thumping of feet on the wooden deck. The sunlight sparkled on the water and men laughed.

I stood away from them and only tapped my foot a little. How I would have loved to dance as well.

Catherine is no better.

le 15 juillet 1666

Many flying fish jumped out of the water and land-ed on the deck. The captain says that something very large, perhaps a shark, must have been hunting them. The sailors cleaned and cooked the fish, and Catherine ate a little. It did not stay down for long. I know in my heart that she would feel much better in the sunshine, but she can barely stand.

le 16 juillet 1666

Catherine now has a fever. So do many of the other girls. It is more than seasickness, I fear.

le 17 juillet 1666

The moaning of the sick girls fills the air. Several of them were hot and flushed this morning, and now all burn with fevers.

I cannot sleep. Catherine is very ill, and there is nothing at all I can do so soothe her.

le 18 juillet 1666

Celine died this morning, and so did Lise, just at sunset. They say the others are very weak. Catherine barely stirs when I call to her, but surely she will recover.

Surely.

le 20 juillet 1666

My sister is dead. Père Denis blessed her with the holy oil of the sick, and so she is in heaven with Maman and Papa.

I did not want to write of this. I did not ever want to write again and would have thrown this diary into the ocean, but if I do not set these words down on paper, then who will remember my sister?

I sat alone with Catherine for a long while until someone knocked and said it was time. Then I washed her face and hands and combed her hair. I kissed her good-bye. She was so cold.

I could not pull the sheet up over her face, so the captain did it. They picked her up, set her on a sheet of canvas, and then set a cannon ball near the bottom. A sailor folded the canvas around Catherine and began to sew it shut. I could not watch.

Madame and Monsieur stood on deck with me. Père Denis said the prayers before they dropped Catherine over the side. My eyes were closed, but I heard the splash. When I opened them, there was nothing but the sea.

le 22 juillet 1666

They tell me that eight of the girls died, one by one. So did four of the men. By the mercy of *le bon Dieu*, all five of the Maries were spared and are slowly recovering.

Of them all, only Catherine matters to me.

le 23 juillet 1666

I am so alone. I cannot weep.

le 26 juillet 1666

I stood at the rail of the ship this morning holding Papa's journal close to my chest. They leave me be. I know that Catherine is in heaven with Maman and Papa. I wondered how it would feel to slip under that water. I cannot swim. Would I be afraid? I felt so very lonely.

Then I heard footsteps. It was Monsieur Aubry.

"When my dear wife Sesi died," he said, "I wanted to die myself. I thought leaving New France might help, but running from my grief did not help at all." His voice was soft and kind. He spoke for a long while. It is strange. I do not know him and I can barely recall what he said, but somehow I felt a little better.

"Your book, mademoiselle," he said finally. "You should take it below so that the rain does not mark its cover." Clouds now covered the sky and it was beginning to sprinkle.

I explained that it was my papa's journal. That he had been a scholar and a natural philosopher. That it was his life's work, but he had not lived to see it published. It had been wet many times when Papa was out studying one thing or another. Still, I tucked it more closely under my cloak.

"I have seen you writing in your own journal in the past, mademoiselle. Perhaps you will take up where he left off. It would be a fitting testimony to him. And to your sister as well, may she rest in peace."

I could not answer.

le 27 juillet 1666

Alone in our cabin, I cried tonight at last. I held Minette in my arms, for she is all I have now, and I wept into her fur. She mewed a little, for I squeezed her too tightly.

Ah, Catherine, Papa, how I miss you both. The loneliness is like something alive, eating at me. It is the first thing in my mind as I wake each morning, and the last thought that is with me when I finally sleep at night. But if that is the only way I can keep you both close to me, I will suffer it, though it hurts so.

Monsieur Aubry is correct. If I write, then I will keep your memories alive.

le 28 juillet 1666

I spent an hour with Kateri today. She is dreadfully thin. I am as well, I suppose, since my clothing hangs on me, but I have not much appetite. The food has become unpleasant, with only salt pork, cabbage and the hard ship's biscuits to eat now.

Minette caught a rat today. Her appetite is good.

le 29 juillet 1666

I am weary of the ocean and the wretched bells. Each day is the same. How I long to see a field, a house, or even a blade of grass. I cannot help but wonder what will become of me, but I dare not think of that.

le 4 août 1666

I now know. Monsieur Deschamps came to me as I stood by the rail. I should take Catherine's place, he said. It is somewhat irregular, but all I need do is agree and I will become a *fille à marier*.

Let me think, I begged him. Give me time.

"You have until we reach New France, mademoiselle," he told me, and his voice sounded as though he was doing business, discussing the price of a chicken or a bolt of cloth.

I nearly burst into tears, but I would not let him see my weakness.

"*Excusez-moi*, Monsieur Deschamps." It was Monsieur Aubry. "You distress Mademoiselle St. Onge. She is my daughter's friend. Therefore you distress me." There was a fierceness in his tone that made Monsieur Deschamps step back.

"*Pardonnez-moi*," Monsieur Deschamps answered stiffly. "But she has few options." Then he bowed and went below. I fear he is correct, and it sickens me.

le 7 août 1666

This evening I spoke for a long while with Monsieur Aubry. Rather, he spoke while Kateri and I listened.

"Monsieur Deschamps is not correct, mademoiselle. You have many options. You know people in the town, mademoiselle. Kateri has told me. The Lecôtés? I have heard of them. Perhaps you may marry their son." I began to protest, but he put up his hand. "Mademoiselle, there are worse things than marriage to a decent man. Or you may return to France."

I said that I could not go back to France.

"You need not. Kateri tells me that you have a relative in Montréal?"

Kateri smiled. What else had she told him? I wondered, before I answered. "She is the widow Madame Barbe Moitié," I finally said.

He laughed at that and said, "*Quelle surprise!* Madame Moitié is an acquaintance of mine. She is a good woman. You might work for her, if marriage does not immediately suit you."

I suppose that I should have been cross that his laughter was directed at me. Instead, I did not mind at all. It is the first time I have seen him smile and heard his laughter. It is a deep, rumbling sound, for his voice is low. Later Kateri said that she has not heard him laugh like that in a very long time.

le 10 août 1666

The days grow steadily cooler. Even when the sun shines, the air is brisk to the point of unpleasantness.

le 14 août 1666

I am tired today, for I could not sleep last night, having wakened in the dark from the saddest dream. I dreamed of Catherine and could not see her face.

Tomorrow is the feast day of the Assumption of the Virgin Mary. At mass, I shall pray for Catherine with all my heart.

Séraphin says that he can smell land. I smell only the ocean and the stink of the ship if I am below. Kateri smells nothing either, but Monsieur Aubry agrees with Séraphin. I hope that we reach land quickly, and I told Monsieur Aubry that I could not wait to see Montréal.

le 18 août 1666

It was the feast day today of Sainte Hélène, after whom I was named. Fourteen years ago I was born. Once, at home, there would have been a small celebration after mass, and a special meal as well. Perhaps mussels. They have always been my favourite. Papa, Catherine and I would have walked through the garden and talked of happy things.

I have left far more than my girlhood behind me today.

le 21 août 1666

Today we are in fog. It surrounds us like a wet, grey blanket. There is not much wind and so the ship moves slowly. Water patters everywhere, dropping from the lines and sails. I pulled the hood of my cloak up and held it closely around my neck, but still the dampness reached in.

The sailors and the captain are wary. One man rings a bell. Another blows a horn. That is to warn any ship near to us that we are here. Men are in the rigging, peering out into the greyness, searching for other vessels and for what Monsieur Aubry says are huge mountains of ice. They sometimes drift down from the north, even at this time of year. The ice mountains are dreadfully dangerous to the ship, and all care must be taken to steer clear of them.

le 24 août 1666

The fog persisted into the evening yesterday. Séraphin said a ship's bell was heard in the night, but the sailors saw nothing. No ice mountains have been sighted, either. I would like to see a mountain of ice, although from a safe distance.

But this morning the fog had lifted, or rather, we were sailing out of it. I watched it disappear behind us. Then Séraphin cried, "Land! I see land."

I could see nothing. Nor could anyone else who stood on the deck. Séraphin was high up in the rigging. How I wish I could have done the same thing. When he came back down, he said again that land was in the distance.

"New France!" I cried.

Séraphin shook his head. "Mademoiselle, it is only Newfoundland, a large island. All around here are the fishing grounds. New France is far inside the country," he explained. "There is a long way to go as yet."

The captain sent Séraphin below to bring up a map, what they call a chart, and yes, it was true. My heart sank. How much longer?

le 25 août 1666

Birds!

This morning the most beautiful thing happened. It cheered my heart and moved me deeply. It began with one small bird, a sort of finch. Papa would have known what it was, although I have not ever seen a bird like it in France.

Then another and another until the entire ship was covered with them. They perched in the rigging and on the ratlings, or hopped about finding and eating small insects. They even landed on peoples' heads and shoulders, promptly going to sleep. Kateri brought up ship's biscuit and crumbled it for them, but the birds cared more for the weevils that fell out.

Monsieur Aubry says that the birds are beginning to fly south as birds do, and they have chosen the ship on which to stop and rest. Perhaps they think we are an island. What a wonderful thought. Papa would have been so pleased to see it all.

After the evening meal I came back out on deck. Many of the birds had died, perhaps from exhaustion or injury caused by the sailors' feet.

I was unable to sleep well tonight. I woke, my pillow wet with tears, a very sad dream of Catherine's spirit weeping over the dead birds clear in my mind. I lay awake for a long while, more hateful tears dampening my pillow.

Why must death come to ruin whatever happiness I take in something?

le 26 août 1666

Three of the Maries say that their teeth are loose. It is difficult to chew food. We all have boils. We have had no fresh fruit or vegetables for weeks, and even the cabbage is gone. The ship's biscuit is like stone and must be soaked. There are turnips and potatoes for the cattle, but none of us will eat such animal food as potatoes.

le 27 août 1666

I think that if it had not been for Kateri, I might not have found the strength to go on. She has become nearly like a sister to me. We pass as much time together as possible, sitting outside when the weather is fine.

The girls talk ceaselessly of the men they will marry. I have not come to know any of them very well, but they are good girls. None of the Maries are as plump as when we left La Rochelle, but all are in excellent spirits. I cannot help but think of poor Catherine and how she would be looking forward to meeting with her Armand. I must give him the sad news. I do hope that he will not be heartbroken, though I fear he will.

le 28 août 1666

It rained hard early this morning. We set out buckets and basins and the captain has let us use some of the water to wash out our clothing. Until now, any laundry has been done in salt water. That makes the cloth very rough and unpleasant against the skin. We hung our shifts and stockings to dry in the sunshine. It made the ship look amusing. Then we females all sat together in the sunshine and did some mending.

All those weeks ago, it would have seemed shocking to display one's underclothing in such a manner. Now, after living so closely together, it is meaningless. After all, it is only linen.

An idea came to me as we worked. I have not only my chest of garments, but Catherine's as well. The gowns are too fine for either Kateri or me. I could sell them, I suppose, but it hurts to think of that. The shifts would do nicely for Kateri. I know Catherine would not mind.

Marie, the one with the mole near her mouth, and Marie, the one with the freckles, helped me to take up the hems and shorten the sleeves. I felt tears burning in my eyes. Catherine was tall.

Monsieur Aubry was not pleased. He said that his daughter would take no charity. He grew quiet when I explained that my gift was an act of friendship, not charity. I will write exactly what I said to him.

"Is it charity for you to help me find my relative, Madame Moitié? No. Only a kindness. Your daughter is my friend," I said, and I could not keep the exasperation from my voice.

He bowed to me then and made his apology. I do not understand men at all.

le 29 août 1666

During the night we sailed well into what Séraphin says is the St. Lawrence River. I have never seen such a wide river. In fact, it looks precisely like the gulf. The mouth is nearly fifty leagues wide.

There are whales here. Some came close to the ship. They are as white as snow and seem to smile. The sailors fired muskets at them. Séraphin says the whales can be eaten, but the balls missed their targets. The whales dived into the water and disappeared. I would like fresh food as much as anyone else would, but secretly I rejoiced that the whales were not harmed.

le 30 août 1666

Today we can see a shoreline. It is nothing but rocks and trees. I knew that New France is largely a wilderness and that there are only a few towns, but I was not prepared for what lies before me. How can anyone make a home in such a place? Kateri is more excited than ever. I am trying to see the countryside through her eyes and the eyes of her father.

Each night I go to my bed more distressed. I have no idea what lies in my future.

le 31 août 1666

Monsieur Aubry is friendlier now, even to *les filles à marier*. The girls flirt outrageously with him, especially Marie with the freckles. He is an eligible man after all, a rather handsome widower and a person of some substance with his business. It is comical, really, to see how they practise upon him. He is good-natured about it.

"You may flutter your eyelashes all you wish, mademoiselles, but I have no need for a wife," he said to them today.

This gave Monsieur Deschamps a shock. I could see it in the way he lifted his eyebrows and twirled the ends of his moustaches furiously.

"Are you above the law, monsieur?" he asked. "Our Intendant, Monsieur Talon, has decreed that all men must be married or lose their licences to trade for furs. You do trade, I have heard."

Monsieur Aubry said nothing. I could have sworn that sparks flew between them, but perhaps it was only lightning. I think it will storm.

le 3 septembre 1666

There was thunder in the night, and I could hear the sound of heavy rain pelting upon the deck. The morning saw no end to this, and so I was unable to spend my accustomed time outside. Besides, the weather has turned very cool, as they say it does so quickly in New France.

Some of the girls sat together and mended stockings. Two dressed each other's hair with ribbons. I chose to return to my little cabin. Sometimes their chattering makes my head ache.

I heard a knock at the door and I asked who was there. It was Kateri. She had something in a basket. It was balls of wool with which she is weaving garters for her father. She does this most cleverly with only her fingers. All the Mohawk girls learn to do it, she told me. Minette thought that batting about balls of wool was nearly as much fun as catching rats. The second makes me shiver.

I had my *lucet*. Kateri wove her garter and I worked at making cord. We spent the afternoon most pleasantly and quietly. One does not need to talk all the while. Sometimes silence, especially the sort of silence that can comfortably grow between friends, is precious.

I wonder where Catherine would have been more content. *La pauvre* Catherine. I will say an extra decade of the rosary tonight for the repose of her soul.

I wonder at something Kateri said, that all Mohawk girls learn the finger weaving. Does she think of herself as Mohawk then? It would be impolite to ask.

le 6 septembre 1666

Monsieur Deschamps pressed me again, this time through Madame Laurent as I took the air on deck with Kateri. She was not unkind, but still, her words did unsettle me.

"Your sister was a *fille à marier*, Hélène. The King paid for her passage on this ship and for this you owe him a debt. Will you not consider taking your sister's place? The King needs his young women to marry and bear children so that New France will be peopled."

I scarcely knew how to answer except to mumble that yes, I would consider it. That seemed to satisfy her. Madame Laurent bid me *bonjour* and walked away.

I have no one to ask for advice.

le 8 septembre 1666

As he does each week, Père Denis heard the confessions of all the girls this morning. Then they attended mass, their souls pure and clean. I did neither, for I feel in my very soul that God abandoned me when Catherine died. Strange looks were cast my way but no one said a word. They continue to leave me to myself.

le 9 septembre 1666

All this time there has been only the ship and we who are on her. There have been trees, rocks and birds, but today we saw people. Our ship was sailing against the current with a strong breeze behind her. Suddenly, three canoes came into sight, moving as quickly as though there were no current at all. In them were Indians, who were more unusual than any men I have ever set my eyes upon. There were ten men or so in the three vessels that Séraphin said were war canoes. *Les sauvages*, he called the men.

I will admit that my heart gave a thump when I heard the words war canoes. Sometimes in recent days I have heard the men talking when they think we cannot hear them. They speak of attacks and kidnappings, the taking of prisoners and such. My mouth grew dry to think that the Indians in those canoes might attack us.

Seeing my nervousness, Kateri said to me, "You need not fear them. They are only Micmac hoping to trade."

It was true. The canoes came quite close to the ship. The men in them laughed and called out in their own tongue. They seemed welcoming enough in spite of the terrible war clubs with which they were armed. They wore barely any clothing, only a length of cloth over their loins that Kateri said was a breechcloth. She confided that her papa often wears one. I will try not to think about that.

No one was able to understand what the Indians said, but their intent was clear. One held up a haunch of meat. Two others each waved a brace of ducks over his head. The meat was passed up, and a sailor reached down and passed a dark green bottle to them.

I have no idea why I looked at Monsieur Aubry's face at that moment. I would have thought he should be happy that we were to have fresh meat for the cook pots. Instead he scowled and his face was angry. I heard the stomping of his feet as he went below. He would not touch a bit of that meat, and neither would Kateri.

"They traded brandy for the meat," she told me later. "It is against the law here, but still some do it. Papa hates to see it happen."

I myself ate nothing tonight, but not because of the brandy. I do not feel well at all.

le 13 septembre 1666

I have wakened, and if I do not write quickly I shall fall asleep again. I have been ill. Madame Laurent tells me that three days passed before the fever broke and that last night Père Denis nearly blessed me with holy oil, since they thought it was possible that I would die. It seems that when he implored me to make my last confession I turned my face away. Madame Laurent says that she is certain it was only the fever talking.

Kateri came to visit me. She says that the other girls speak of my refusal of the sacrament as a sin. They cross themselves endlessly.

"Papa did the same when Maman died. He blamed *le bon Dieu* for a long while," she told me. "My Mohawk grandmother and grandfather say that all things pass."

I was very sleepy and weak. But I know that I heard her speak of her grandparents. Now here is something new, but I am far too weary to think about it. I must put down the quill before I drop it and add yet another stain to this coverlet.

le 14 septembre 1666

I am weary beyond words as I write this. I felt strong enough to come out into the sunshine for a while today, and I could see a town in the distance. It is the city of Québec. I do not know what I expected. Papa always believed that one must not expect too much and then one will not be disappointed. I see the point he tried to make to me, but I cannot help it. This town could have turned out to be a single hovel with a pig standing next to it and I would have been overjoyed to view a place where people live. I expected a good deal from New France, and this place, standing alone in such a wilderness, has moved me deeply.

As the ship drew closer I could see that the site chosen for Québec is magnificent and imposing. There are tall cliffs, and above the trees and the river rises a large hill. I picked Minette up so that she could see it.

"It is called Cap Diamant."

It was Monsieur Aubry. He had come up beside me to where I stood at the ship's rail. Monsieur Aubry, I have learned, is able to walk very quietly so that he is there before you even notice him. The other men on the ship wear shoes of stout leather, but he now wears what are called moccasins, which are slippers of moose skin made in the Indian style.

He did not look at me as he talked. Kateri joined us. He put his arm around his daughter, but he spoke almost as though neither of us was there. It had been an Indian village once, when the explorer Cartier first saw it, he went on. Stadacona. Then Samuel de Champlain, long dead, built a trading post. The trading post became this town of Québec.

He stopped speaking for a moment and glanced at me. "The fur trade drives it all, mademoiselle. Commerce and marriage, war and peace are all determined by the fur trade. See the canoes?" He gestured to the many distant vessels that were all making their way to Québec.

The canoes were very low in the water. At that time, it meant little to me and Monsieur Aubry could see that.

"Furs, mademoiselle. They are filled with hundreds of furs. The town will be busy indeed, and those who trade here will be tired tonight."

When he said tired, I realized how tired I was. I excused myself and went down to my cabin to rest and to think. The fur trade drives it all, he said. How will this trading drive *my* life?

le 15 septembre 1666

We have anchored in the river some distance from what Séraphin calls the Lower Town. The sun shines brightly, there are no clouds in the sky and the air is remarkably sweet and crisp. Canoes filled with Indians or coureurs de bois — which is what they call the men who go out to trade with the Indians here — carry large bales of furs past us. Many of the men in the canoes do not even glance at the ship. They stare straight ahead at their goal, which seems to be the town itself. I cannot help but do the same thing. We are to go ashore soon for supplies and an outing.

le 16 septembre 1666

I have made my decision. The seriousness of what I have done keeps me from sleep, so yet again I write. It soothes my mind. I will take Catherine's place as a *fille à marier*. When I told Kateri this, her eyes grew wide and she excused herself. Of course, I knew that she was running off to tell her father. I was surprised that he took only a few minutes to find me out on the deck.

"You are certain?" he asked in concern. "I mean to say, there is nothing wrong at all with agreeing to become a *fille à marier*, mademoiselle. Many good marriages have come out of it. The wrong lies in your being pressed."

I assured him that the choice was mine. I said that my future was too uncertain and at least in this way, if I had no other choice, with a dowry I would be viewed as a possible wife. Without one, there would be no hope. I would not marry in haste, and I did intend to put it off as long as possible. I added that that should not be a problem, since I was not exactly the sort of girl men looked at twice.

Monsieur Aubry laughed aloud. It is fortunate that it does not make me angry, since he persists in doing this.

He wiped his eyes and said, "Merci, mademoiselle. I can count on you for bringing cheer into my day. You are correct, of course. You are not the sort of girl a man looks at twice."

I felt a strange hollow pang in my belly that he should agree, but then he added, "Many times, perhaps, but never just twice." He bowed and went below.

Now that I think on it, I am not certain exactly what he meant. I do enjoy making him laugh, though. It is difficult being alone, so difficult without Catherine, but the sound of his laughter helps a bit.

le 17 septembre 1666

I spoke with Madame Laurent and Monsieur Deschamps. I am now a *fille à marier*.

I did not feel one bit different as I dressed this morning, putting on a clean *chemise* and my Sunday gown of deep green wool. The sleeves are long and the sun was shining, so I did not bother with a cloak.

The Maries were already on the deck when I came out. My, how splendid they looked in their finest clothing and their hair prettily dressed. I suppose that when one is looking for a husband it is important to look appealing at all times. Even Marie with the missing front tooth was particularly lovely. She smiled so warmly and laughed so much, that a person barely noticed the space in her smile. The Maries could not compete with Monsieur Deschamps, though, who wore fashionably full breeches and shoes with ribbons.

Two of the ship's boats were lowered to the water and we were helped down into them. Monsieur Deschamps rode with the captain and the girls in one boat. I went into the other with Madame Laurent, Kateri and her father. Séraphin was with us as well. In both boats were several merchants who intend to go no further than Québec. All were armed. One had a blunderbuss and the others had muskets, as, I saw, did Monsieur Aubry. At the last moment, Minette, who had somehow escaped from my cabin, leaped down into my lap and settled herself there. If I was to have an adventure, then she would as well. Séraphin handed me a piece of rope and I tied it onto her collar. He always seems to have a piece of rope about him.

"Is this not exciting," cried Séraphin. Monsieur Aubry smiled. He did not want to show it, I think, but he was as eager as any of us.

I called to Séraphin that I agreed. I could not help myself. After all this while on the ship, the thought of setting my feet onto dry land was wonderful. At that moment, Madame Laurent leaned over and pinched me on the arm. She whispered something about my behaviour being unbecoming to a *fille à marier.* I was so startled that I could not say a word, only sat there rubbing my arm. She had seemed so kind until now, but some people do change when their dignity is threatened.

Then my temper rose. I have not written of this, for it is not really something one wishes to set down on paper for the entire world to see, but I have a hot temper. Papa used to say I am fiery just as Maman was when she was a young girl. Did she fight the same battles with her temper as I do?

My temper won. I could not control myself. I stuck my tongue out at Madame Laurent.

She was just reaching out to pinch me again when Monsieur Aubry said sweetly, "You had best hold onto the boat's rail, Madame Laurent. Think of how cold the water would be if some person were to accidentally jostle against you and you should take a tumble. Can you swim, Madame Laurent?"

Madame turned an unpleasant shade of purple, opened and shut her mouth several times, just like the carp in the pond at *Le Cadeau,* and then grasped the rail tightly.

I thought no one had seen. The Maries were chattering, Kateri was peering intently at the town, and the sailors were rowing and steering. My eyes chanced to meet those of Monsieur Aubry. He said nothing, only nodded to me, and I knew that he had seen Madame Laurent's fingers at work.

The little boats stopped at the shore, sailors tossed ropes to men waiting there, and we were all helped out. I held my skirts carefully out of the way, remembering what Monsieur Aubry had said about the coldness of the water. I for one did not wish to be jostled or tumble in.

Though I have a temper I tend not to bear grudges, and so I held out my hand to Madame Laurent when she stumbled a bit. She seemed surprised, and muttered something about what a kind girl I was, but in truth, I had also reached out to her because I found it very difficult to stand. What had seemed to be solid earth was not. I could feel the world moving around me just as though I was still at sea on *Le Chat Blanc*.

Many of the others were doing the same. *Les filles à marier* held onto each other and even Monsieur Deschamps nearly lost his fine beaver hat.

"Walking will help," Monsieur Aubry laughed. "You will have to become accustomed to land again."

I set Minette down, for she was struggling, doubtlessly anxious to set her paws down upon the soil of New France. When I did, she staggered as badly as I did. We made our way up the street though it was the strangest sensation I have ever felt. I could have vowed that with each step the street should be rising in a wave just as the sea would.

There were many men here at what is called the

Lower Town. Some were Indians who had been removing bales of furs from their canoes. I would learn later that some were local merchants, traders and farmers who either lived here or who had come into the town on some business or other. All work had stopped. There was quiet talk and not so quiet laughter amongst some of the men as they assessed each of us, including me, very frankly.

That was a shock, I must say. Until that moment, I had not really felt myself to be one of *les filles à marier*. I did not feel above them, only separate from them. I had not come to New France to marry. I had not spent all these weeks talking about a prospective husband. I did not dress in my best so that I would be appealing to a single man. And yet, the men assumed I had. It unsettled my mind.

No one was rude. The presence of Monsieur Deschamps seemed to assure that. One of the men, a prosperous looking sort with a plump belly, took Monsieur Deschamps aside and asked him something. I strained my ears but could not hear them.

The man shook his head, shrugged his shoulders and called out, "*C'est dommage*. These young women are meant for the lucky fellows in Montréal. We may only pray a few might be persuaded to change their minds, as is their right, and settle here."

Monsieur Deschamps made his apologies, and led

us on to an inn where we were to take refreshment. I looked around for Kateri and her father, but they had disappeared into the crowd. Séraphin was already at work loading supplies the captain had ordered.

The fresh bread and cheese were lovely, and the innkeeper did not mind a cat in his inn, but it would have been more a pleasure to have shared the meal with Kateri.

Later, we were walking down the street, making our way back to the boats. Again the men watched as we passed, all very polite and jolly, all clearly in search of a wife. Marie with the mole beside her mouth was flirting with a farmer. People laughed, a man began a song, and it seemed quite pleasant.

Then someone asked Monsieur Deschamps about the girl with the snapping black eyes. Kateri stood near the water's edge with her father. She smiled and waved to me. It was clearly her the man meant.

Monsieur Deschamps's eyebrows lifted, he touched a handkerchief to his lips, and he answered the man in a quiet voice. It was not quiet enough to escape my ears, though.

Bâtarde. Mongrel, he called her. She is mixed blood. You do not want that one, monsieur, when there are so many strapping French girls from which to choose, all *filles à marier*.

The man made a joke about how it was the girls

who would likely do the choosing, but by then the afternoon had been spoilt for me.

le 20 septembre 1666

I am writing this in a small inn called *L'Érable*. It is named after the maple trees that grow so abundantly here. I am not alone. Kateri is sleeping in the bed next to me, the covers pulled up nearly over her head.

A terrible thing has happened. Last night there was a fire in the ship's galley. I was sleeping soundly with Minette curled at my feet, when I was wakened by shouts outside my cabin. A woman screamed, footsteps sounded as someone ran by, and the door was pulled open. Madame Laurent stood there in her nightdress, a shawl over her shoulders, her eyes terrified. Smoke swirled around her.

"You must get out, Hélène!" she screamed. "Get out!" And she ran from my sight.

I snatched up my cloak and pulled it over my shoulders, and then I stood very still for a moment. Everything I owned was here in this little cabin. My chest of clothing, and Catherine's, the bedding from home. What should I carry out? I took the two things that were the most important to me, the cloth bag that held this diary and Papa's journal, and

Minette, who had made herself very flat in her extreme fear, poor thing. When I picked her up she trembled horribly.

I made my way through the ship and out onto the deck. Never had I been so grateful to breathe fresh air into my lungs. I leaned against the rail for a moment, coughing and gasping. Sailors ran everywhere. They passed buckets of water to each other in a line that led to the galley.

"It looks worse than it is," Séraphin shouted up. He was in the boat alongside the ship where Madame Laurent, Monsieur Deschamps and the Maries all sat crammed in with our priest. "But you must go ashore for the sake of safety." He reached up for my hand.

Monsieur Aubry called out just then. His arm was around Kateri, who shivered as I did. He was carrying a musket. Surely there was room for her, he said. Monsieur Deschamps shook his head and said something about it being too crowded. Wait for the other boat to be brought around.

"Come, Hélène," Madame Laurent pleaded. "We have saved you a place."

I cannot recall whether it was cold or heat that I felt inside myself. Anger does that to me.

The Maries insisted that they could squeeze together and make themselves very small, but they were ignored.

I would wait as well, I answered, and I turned my back on the boat. I slipped my hand into Kateri's. She had tears in her eyes now, tears of shame at how she had been treated. I leaned my forehead against hers and battled my own angry tears. I heard Séraphin climb back onto the ship, and then the dipping of the oars as the boat pulled away toward shore.

Someone cheered. The fire was out. I went below to dress presentably, and the stink of the smoke was everywhere. The bedding would have to be washed or aired, and any clothing left out must be washed as well. With a sigh I bundled up my nightdress, stuffed it into the cloth bag and, with Minette in my arms, hurried back onto the deck.

Rowing ashore in the boat, Monsieur Aubry was so enraged he could not speak at first. The Maries' faces had all worn looks of horror when Monsieur Deschamps and Madame Laurent had spoken. I myself did not know what to say to him or to Kateri.

Monsieur Deschamps had taken them all to a house on the grounds of the Ursuline convent. I knew I should excuse myself and follow, but it did not seem right to do so. Instead, I went with Kateri and her father to this inn where he insisted he pay for my room. I suppose I shall be in total disfavour when I see Madame Laurent and Monsieur Deschamps again tomorrow, but I am far too tired to think of that now. Sleep calls.

le 22 septembre 1666

If I do not set down the events of this afternoon carefully here, I may believe that I imagined them. Short Marie and Marie with the freckles are to be married next Monday, since the priests here prefer that day for weddings. It happened that quickly. New France is truly an unpredictable place. There was no courtship or expressions of fondness. If I had not seen it myself, I would not have believed that marriage could be like this.

We had left the inn to return to the ship. Monsieur Deschamps, Madame Laurent and the Maries were already standing near the water. Two men, strangers, were there as well.

Short Marie was asking one of the gentlemen questions. Marie with the freckles was doing the same with the other.

"How large is your house?"

"How many chickens did you say you have?"

"Your cow. Is her milk rich with cream?"

"You are a widower with six children, monsieur. I trust they are all well behaved." On it went. Finally, Monsieur Deschamps walked with the couples to the notary.

"The marriage contracts must be drawn up, you see," Madame Laurent told me as the rest of us returned to the ship. "Lucky girls. Now they need not travel on to Montréal."

I know short Marie and Marie with the freckles have found what they wanted. Each will have a husband and a life of security, but I think it might have been more pleasant if they had proceeded a bit more slowly. I said nothing of my thoughts to anyone, though, since the other girls seem so pleased for our friends.

le 23 septembre 1666

More unsettling news. *Le Chat Blanc* will not sail on to Montréal. Ships usually do not sail that far anyway since there is no real harbour, but the captain had agreed. Now he has reversed his decision, and nothing Monsieur Deschamps says will change his mind. Besides, the captain said, the galley is more badly damaged than first thought and repairs must be undertaken. There will be this one last night aboard the ship and then we and our possessions must go ashore. He has agreed to take a letter to France for me when his ship sails. Cousin Pierre must know of Catherine's death.

The idea of sailing back did not please the crew. It is late in the year and the voyage back will be cold and difficult. Some say they will remain here. There are sailors eager to return to France, however, and so they will take their places.

The remaining Maries were frantic at the thought that we were stranded at Québec. So was I, although I hid it as well as I could. How would we reach Montréal now?

Monsieur Aubry laughed at this. "By canoe, of course. It is the way the Indians have always travelled."

"You must come with us," Kateri insisted.

Monsieur Deschamps did not like that at all. Before I could say a word he was carrying on about chaperones. To do such a thing would ruin my reputation.

"I will only permit this if we all travel together," Monsieur Deschamps insisted. "Mademoiselle St. Onge is a *fille à marier*, I remind you."

Monsieur Aubry leaned on his musket and hesitated. His dislike for Monsieur Deschamps was quite evident at that moment. But he agreed, and even graciously offered to make the arrangements. At once, the girls began to chatter and plan.

I went to Monsieur Aubry and thanked him for his kindness to us.

"Make no mistake, mademoiselle," he said. "I would leave Monsieur Deschamps behind in an instant. His sort angers me. This I have done for the

sake of the women and, of course, for your sake."
Seeing how I blushed, he added, "I do not mean to be
forward, mademoiselle. Kateri values your friendship greatly."

I valued hers as well, I told him.

As I lie here writing, it occurs to me that perhaps
I might have added that Monsieur Aubry's own
friendship could mean something to me as well,
were it to be offered.

le 24 septembre 1666

I write this at yet another setting, one that could not
be more different from the ship or the inn.

I was almost sad to leave our vessel this morning,
since it has been my home all these months. I
watched it grow smaller as we rowed toward shore.
I will miss it in some ways. It was crowded and it
stank, especially after the fire, but it had become so
very familiar. Even Minette seemed to feel as I did,
making herself into a small shape in my lap. Once
we were deposited on the shore, the boats went back
for our chests.

This time I followed the other girls to the
Ursuline convent where short Marie and Marie
with the freckles had remained behind. I made certain to embrace Kateri before I did this, and to whis-
per in her ear that I would see her soon. I curtsied

to Monsieur Aubry and he gave a little bow. Then he went off with Kateri to arrange for the canoes that will carry us to Montréal.

It was a long walk up the hill. Some of the sisters were working in the garden nearby. I could see rows of cabbages and vines bearing squash. There was the smell of bread baking. It made the water come into my mouth and made me think of home. One of the women looked up and smiled.

Mère Marie de l'Incarnation, who founded this convent, was so kind as to give us rooms for the night. They seem happy, these women, serving *le bon Dieu* through their prayers and teaching. There is a school here, after all, for the girls of the towns-people and for the Indian girls as well. Mère Marie de l'Incarnation speaks the language of the Indians, Madame Laurent has told us, though she says she cannot understand why one would bother to learn.

I, of course, do not agree with her, although I keep that to myself, not wishing to be pinched yet again. I must ask Kateri about her education. I have no idea whether she can even read. How sad that would be if she cannot.

le 25 septembre 1666

The chests were carried up today and there was a bustle of activity. The weddings will be in two days, and both short Marie and Marie with the freckles are excited beyond words. They each now have a little brass ring from their future husbands. Jesuit rings, the sisters call them. They wear the rings on the third finger of their left hand, as they should, for the vein in that finger leads directly to the heart. Not that there has been much romance so far.

The wedding *fête* preparations took nearly all day. There would be a turkey, squash, bread and cheese. Monsieur Aubry came up to speak to Monsieur Deschamps, and when he and Kateri saw me at work they both laughed aloud. I was covered in feathers.

It is the first turkey I have ever plucked, I explained. Chickens are a simple matter compared to such a large creature.

Everything here seems large.

le 26 septembre 1666

Happy news. Séraphin is leaving the ship and will come with us to Montréal. There he will become an *engagé*, signing a contract and working for a tradesman or a farmer. It makes me think. Séraphin will be free in three years if he does this. For me, a marriage will be forever.

le 27 septembre 1666

What a day! I made my confession at last to one of
the priests at the church here. It seemed the proper
thing to do, since I was going to church for the weddings, and, in truth, I felt a weight lift from me.
There is comfort in familiar things. Père Chesne
was kind and understanding.

"Place yourself in the hands of God, my daughter," he whispered. "He will guide you."

The weddings were simple and lovely. We deco-
rated the altar inside the church Notre-Dame-de-
l'Immaculée-Conception with the goldenrod and
asters that grow wild in places down in the Lower
Town. Many witnesses attended the ceremonies,
and everyone dressed as finely as they could for
such an occasion. The brides both wore their clean
Sunday gowns. I had given them each pretty ribbons
from Catherine's trousseau, which made them look
lovely. With their shining eyes and happy smiles,
the Maries hardly needed the ribbons.

I have been to weddings before back in France.
Somehow, this was quite different. There was the
ever-present smell of incense in the church, and the
familiar hymns *"Te Deum"* and *"Reis Glorios."* The
mass was the same, and the wedding vows
exchanged in the same manner as always, but to me
there was such a feeling of hope. The fact that the

church was a small and simple thing built to withstand any sort of attack did not seem to matter at all. I might have felt grief rise up in me, yet mercifully it did not. I felt only a quiet happiness for the couples.

Would I find such happiness for myself?

The priest handed each of the grooms a ring. These were the same Jesuit rings I had seen before. The rings, now blessed, were slipped upon the fingers of the Maries. I cannot see how it might have been possible for them to look happier, but they did. When it all ended, Marie with the freckles had become Madame LaForêt, and short Marie had been transformed into Madame Doner. I must think of them in that way always now, for they are married women.

"*C'est dommage*," said Madame Laurent mournfully when we left the church. "Neither they and their husbands, nor any of you girls, are eligible to receive the twenty *livres* that the Intendant Monsieur Talon gives newly wedded couples as a gift from the King. You must be a girl of less than sixteen or a man of less than twenty for that." Then she turned to me. "Only you, Hélène, shall have it." What a thought.

The wedding *fête* was enjoyable. The men drank beer, unpleasant-smelling beer that they make here from fir needles. There was all of the food and then dancing, in spite of the fact that the priests do not like dancing at all. The *contredanses* and *gigues à deux* were all such fun. There was no shortage of partners, for everyone was eager to share in the festivities. There were fiddles, a recorder and even a hurdy gurdy. What a happy sound they made. Even Monsieur Aubry set his musket aside and danced, though at first I thought he would not.

"He has not danced since Maman died," Kateri explained. "There are so many things he does not do because they remind him of her. She loved to dance at the Mohawk feasts. It is wonderful to see him taking pleasure in such things again." She tilted her head to one side thoughtfully and added, "You and Maman would have liked one another, I think."

I suspect I would have liked this woman, Sesi. How much she was loved! There are not many things more important than being able to inspire love.

There was hopeful talk of peace with the Indians. Soldiers of the Carignan-Salières Regiment came from France last year to protect the settlements, I heard one man say. Mohawk villages were burned, he added. At this he smiled and laughed most unpleasantly.

I know nothing of war, but I cannot see how such a thing could beget peace. Mère Marie de l'Incarnation left everything behind, even her son, to come here and help the priests bring the word of *le bon Dieu* to this place. She learned the language of the Indians. She founded the Ursuline convent. She welcomed we *filles à marier* with such generosity.

Surely such kindness as hers may help beget peace in time.

le 28 septembre 1666

A thing I feared has indeed happened, and I nearly do not want to record it here. Perhaps if I begin with the day's pleasant events, the words will come more easily.

The wedding *fête* lasted until very late. I slept long this morning and therefore missed mass. I saw some cold looks directed at me by a few of the sisters.

I felt the need to escape. After breakfast, I walked down to the Lower Town with Marie who never speaks. Minette walked between us, her tail in the air. Marie never speaks but she listens nicely and she is excellent company. I cannot tell whether it is shyness or extreme conservativeness that keeps her lips sealed, but that does not matter. She smiles and nods. She has a lovely smile and big blue eyes, and I noticed that many men look at her with admiration.

Kateri was there with her father, who was working quite industriously. He had arranged for us to journey in large canoes like the ones the Indians use. Men were loading bales of goods, kegs and supplies into them.

"Come and see," called Kateri, when she saw me staring. "This is how we will travel."

I came close and looked down into one of the canoes. It was perhaps a bit more than three *toises* in length, longer than three tall men lying down, and made of birchbark that covered a frame of wood. The walls of it were so thin that I could not help but wonder how safe such a thing might be. My concern must have shown on my face.

"You can see it is very strong, mademoiselle," Monsieur Aubry assured me. "What is not held together by friction is held by spruce roots, and it is sealed with animal fat mixed with spruce gum."

Minette leaped in, sat down and begin washing her face. How we all laughed at that. I thanked Monsieur Aubry politely when he handed her back.

"Soon enough, cat," he said. "We leave early in the morning."

It was then that it happened. A grey-haired man who looked thin and worn stopped directly in front of me. Seven children, from a girl nearly my age to the infant she held in her arms, were behind him. They looked at me with curious eyes. The man did not wait, but began to make his case immediately.

He was a widower with a small house, some geese, a milk cow and a farm. He was strong, and, as I could see, a good father. He needed a wife. I was a *fille à marier*, was I not? The contract could be quickly drawn up if I was willing.

My mouth hung open and I could feel the hot flush rising up my neck. Again it was as though I were a cabbage in the marketplace, just waiting for someone to offer a price for it. Finally I just stared at the ground and shook my head. As gently as possible I met his eyes, thanked him for his offer and declined.

"I must go on to Montréal," I said. "Merci, monsieur."

The man did not seem the least disappointed, which confused me even more. On the other hand, the amusement with which Kateri had watched it all nearly made me cross. I like her far too much to be cross with her. However, if she seemed amused, her father did not.

"You did well, mademoiselle," he said slowly. "You were kind to him. Even a small measure of kindness is important here." He turned back to his work.

Before I left, Kateri whispered to me that I should not wear a *corps* tomorrow. It would be uncomfortable, as I would be sleeping in my gown until we reached Montréal. I glanced once at her father to see if he had any idea what she was telling me. He clearly did. I must ask Kateri if the advice was hers or his.

le 29 septembre 1666

It has been a long and tiring day. I rose in the dark and dressed by the light of a single tallow candle. It is Michelmas, the feast of Saint Michael the Archangel, and we would have attended mass, but there was no time. Men were waiting outside the convent to carry our chests to the Lower Town.

We walked down ourselves after a meagre breakfast of bread, cheese and water. It was foggy, and with each step swirls of grey parted like smoke. My cloak grew damp and little wisps of my hair began to curl. At the shore the men in the canoes seemed impatient to leave. It is the best part of the day, one laughed. How can you see to tell? laughed another. At least they were cheerful.

Our group was split amongst six canoes. It was for the sake of the weight, Monsieur Aubrey said. I will not say it was planned, but Séraphin, Kateri and her father were to ride in the same canoe as I. My, what a happy coincidence that was.

Kateri was dressed as warmly as I was. We are both practical and so it was no real surprise. It was Monsieur Aubry who gave me the first of his surprises. I looked from him to Monsieur Deschamps. What a difference there was between them.

Monsieur Deschamps was as elegant as ever, but a transformation had taken place with Monsieur Aubry. Gone was the felt hat and full petticoat breeches. He now wore the same sort of clothing as the other men in the canoe. A heavy *capote* of wool belted with a woven sash covered his upper body. A cap was on his head, and he wore high wool leggings and his moccasins.

He also wore many weapons. He had the musket he is never now without, a knife, and what the Indians call a tomahawk thrust through the sash at his waist. I wondered briefly about the possibility of a breechcloth and put that out of my head.

Then Monsieur Aubry cleared his throat and said, "Mademoiselle, I have a gift."

Monsieur Deschamps's eyebrows raised, all the Maries tittered, and Madame Laurent shook her head. I murmured something about not being able to accept a gift.

"It is not for you, mademoiselle, but for your cat," he explained. "Surely your cat may accept a gift without scandal."

It was a basket with a lid. Minette could sleep inside it on the basket's soft cushion in perfect comfort, and there would be no chance of her falling out of the canoe. Minette crept in, mewed once and curled herself into a ball. The mew meant *merci*, I told Monsieur Aubry. It seemed to please him.

We females were helped into the canoes. I settled myself onto a low chair against which I could lean back. I folded my legs quite comfortably, and covered my lap and Minette's basket with a blanket.

We left Québec, and the men paddled hard as we went up the river. In time the fog lifted, the sun burning it off. The river is such a perfect thing, wide and smooth with clear, deep water. During the day I saw a deer drinking, and what they said was a female moose with an enormous calf.

It seems that if there had been no women in the party, the canoes would not have stopped until nightfall. But there were women, and near noon the canoes were paddled to the shore and we were allowed to go into the bushes. One of the men checked carefully first to make certain there were no plants that cause terrible itching.

Now it is night. I lie here under a canoe, wrapped in blankets, sleeping in my gown. I cannot help but wonder if Madame Laurent and the Maries gave off wearing their *corps*. I passed the advice on to them, and only Madame Laurent now tosses and turns uncomfortably, so I believe that I know the answer. I do wish she would not grunt so.

le 30 septembre 1666

The men sing. It helps them to keep a rhythm as they paddle, and it is a happy sound. *"En Roulant Ma Boule"* and *"C'est l'Aviron"* ring out repeatedly, sometimes with humorous new words added. Although they could not paddle to it, Madame Laurent surprised us all by singing *"Au Clair de la Lune,"* a song by the famous Monsieur Lully who composes for the King at court, and for the thousandth time my thoughts went back to *Le Cadeau*. There was no going back, though, we would only go forward.

Québec seemed like a small, primitive settlement when I first saw it. Now I understand that it is a bastion of civilization in this wilderness. For a moment, I felt fear beginning to grow within me, but then I tried to see the land as Papa would have. It is so empty and beautiful here. The trees are the largest I have ever seen. When I said that aloud, Monsieur Aubry, who paddles behind me, informed me that these trees have never been cut.

They have grown here forever, I marvelled, for I was deeply moved. "Think of the wonder of such beauty that has never been touched," I said, and looked back at him to ask if he agreed.

He was watching me carefully, a thoughtful look in his expression. "Many cannot see beyond the hardships here, mademoiselle. Yes, I agree. Hopefully you will always see New France in the same way," he answered. "She will offer you many challenges, you know."

Tonight we will sleep under the stars, for the night is so warm, and a challenge in its own way. I cannot understand the weather here. First it is cold, then it is hot, and one does not know how to dress. It is simpler for the men. They remove what they do not wish to wear. It horrifies Madame Laurent.

le 1 octobre 1666

Monsieur Aubry says that the countryside is rich with food if you know what to eat. If the French would eat like the Indians they would be far more content. He found some shaggy-mane mushrooms in the forest. Those I recognized, for I used to walk in the woods and search for them with Papa after a warm rain. The large white mushroom I did not.

"It is a puffball, mademoiselle," Monsieur Aubry explained. "Delicious."

He had a little lard in which he fried them. I did take a small taste and then a larger serving, for they were quite tasty.

They said back in France that the King is very fond of mushrooms, and that he has them grown for his table. I wonder what he would think of such a thing as a puffball?

le 2 octobre 1666

At midday another canoe joined our party. It was filled with Indians. Kateri grew very excited, and said something to her father in a tongue that I had never heard.

"They are Mohawks," she told me happily. "They call themselves *Kanienkehaka*, the People of the Flint. Not from our village, but from one nearby. Home draws closer, Hélène. They will travel with us up river, they say."

The Mohawks wear only breechcloths. Madame Laurent says it is indecent, and that we should avert our eyes. I, naturally, do not listen. If I avert my eyes, how can I see and then describe it here?

They are muscular men with darkly tanned skin that they rub with grease. Their heads are partly shaved, and some of them wear a narrow piece of deerskin, the hair of which stands up like the mane of a horse. Kateri says this is called a roach. They wear silver earrings, and their skin is covered in blue patterns. Those are tattoos, Monsieur Aubry explained, made by pricking or cutting the skin and then rubbing charcoal onto the bleeding spots. The skin is then stained.

I cannot stop thinking about the Mohawks and the Aubrys. At Québec, the Indians were called *les sauvages,* mainly, Monsieur Aubry has told me, because they are not Catholics. That may be so, but there truly is a savagery and wildness in the appearance of these Mohawks that was at first disturbing. Yet Monsieur Aubry wed a Mohawk woman and so Kateri is half Mohawk. There is nothing savage about either of them. Monsieur Deschamps and Madame Laurent will not even look at the warriors, and they *are* warriors, Kateri tells me. Is there danger? I cannot feel it and Papa always said to trust my feelings. I think I will trust the judgment of Monsieur Aubry for the moment.

le 3 octobre 1666

At last I am in Montréal, where we arrived today. So many things have happened, some happy and some sad, and I shall describe them all.

Last night we girls had heated water to wash our hands and faces behind a screen of blankets we created away from the camp. Four men guarded us, their backs to the shelter. The Mohawks, who had their camp some distance away from ours, seemed to find this entertaining.

This morning we garbed ourselves carefully in our freshest clothing, again behind the screen, and dressed each other's hair. I am not one for curls and frizzing, so my hair was swept up in a tidy *chignon*. I used some of the tortoiseshell pins from Catherine's chest, breathing a little prayer for her.

When we set out it was a beautiful morning. We were less than ten leagues from Montréal. The sun sparkled on the water and lit the trees. They are all colours now, red, orange and yellow, and it looked as though the hills on either side of the river were aflame. I was excited, but under that excitement I felt anxious. How would Armand react to the news of Catherine's death? The Lecôtés were surely kind. They would help me somehow. I set my mind and told myself to deal with it bit by bit. Papa always said to think before I acted. I have never been very good at that, but I could see that I must learn now.

I took Minette out from her travelling basket and put the little collar around her neck. She seemed very happy at that. She knows the collar and leash mean a walk is coming.

She must be a good cat and wash her face, I whispered. She must make a suitable first impression on the Lecôtés.

Soon Montréal was seen in the distance, growing larger and larger. It too wore a coat of coloured trees, the ones on the hill at its centre being especially lovely. A palisade of logs surrounded the town. Soon I could pick out people who were outside the fort, on what I would learn was the common where animals grazed.

My heart thumped hard. I was not the only nervous one. Marie with the mole was telling her rosary beads with her eyes squeezed shut, Marie with the missing front tooth was fanning herself wildly with her handkerchief, and Marie who never speaks was gripping the sides of the canoe so tightly that her fingers were white.

We neared the shore just as the sun was going behind purple clouds. There were many people on the beach.

Monsieur Aubry was explaining something about a fur trading fair when a man on the shore cheered, *"Vive le Roi!"* and then others turned to stare. I could almost feel the air change as excitement swept through them.

"Les filles à marier! Les filles à marier!" The words echoed through the crowd, and men rushed forward to meet our canoes.

The canoes were pulled to the beach and, one by one, we girls and Madame Laurent were helped out with such care you would have thought we were made of the most delicate porcelain. How the men stared at us as we walked through the crowd. They were not rude, only curious and welcoming.

"Now you are for it!" laughed one man, slapping his companion across the shoulders.

"Your days as a free man are over, my friend," called out another.

How some of the men scowled at this.

Madame Laurent explained that some of the men do not wish to marry, but there is no choice. "Ignore them," she said. "Most are willing enough." Then with great authority she announced, "We will take the girls to la Soeur Bourgeoys's house, Monsieur Deschamps. I wish to see them settled, for I will return to Québec in a few days." She turned to us. "You girls will be safe and comfortable with her."

My heart sank. I had no wish to go to la Soeur Bourgeoys's house. I must find the home of the Lecôtés, I told her. But when I said as much, Monsieur Deschamps was firm. I would go with the other girls.

Monsieur Aubry said in a low voice. "Mademoiselle St. Onge may be a *fille à marier*, Monsieur Deschamps, but she has this last responsibility to her sister." He dismissed Monsieur Deschamps as though he were an annoying gnat, and turned to me. "Do not concern yourself about your safety, mademoiselle. I will take you to the Lecôtés. Then I will escort you and your belongings to la Soeur Bourgeoys's house before I take Kateri home to my shop. You may accompany us if you wish, Séraphin. I can provide you with a bed until you find a position."

"Merci, Monsieur Aubry," said Séraphin in great relief.

Monsieur Aubry hired an ox cart. The man who

owned it helped him and Séraphin pile in our chests. Yes, he knew the location of the Lecôté house. It was a fine building.

Minette, who loves high places, jumped up and sat at the very top of the pile. The Indians could not stop laughing and pointing. Kateri squeezed my hand and I gave her a tiny smile. We walked through the palisade and into the town as the man leading the ox chattered to Monsieur Aubry and Séraphin.

The farms and houses I saw that day might have been invisible. My mind was so busy with what I would say to Armand that when the cart stopped, I went on a few steps.

It was a large house, large, at least, by the standards of the town. The Lecôtés were wealthy. How happy Catherine would have been here, I thought. How sad her beloved Armand would be. Kateri took Minette in her arms so that she would not follow. I took a deep breath, smoothed my hair, and walked to the door. I knocked once and waited. Silence.

I had just raised my hand to knock again when a young woman opened the door. She smiled, looked past me at the cart and people who waited on the street and said, "Bonjour, mademoiselle. How may I help you?"

I asked to speak with Armand Lecôté. He was not here, nor was his father, I learned, and so I asked to speak to his mother.

She was, unfortunately, not at home either, the woman said sweetly.

When I explained that I must give a message to Armand Lecôté, she looked surprised.

"You may leave the message with me, mademoiselle," she said. "I, you see, am Armand's wife."

When I then explained that I did not know of Armand's marriage she seemed confused, but she quickly composed herself. How rude of Armand to neglect to write, she said, but then love addles a man's brains sometimes, does it not? Would I care to wait inside and pay my respects to him?

I would not. She could tell Armand, though, that Catherine St. Onge was dead.

"Who was she?" asked Armand's wife in confusion. When I turned away she called out, "I will say a prayer for her soul, mademoiselle."

I walked back to the cart with as much dignity as I could manage, but my face was pale and I could feel the tears wanting to start in my eyes. I would not let myself weep. I took Minette from Kateri and glanced at Monsieur Aubry. There was no pity in his face, and now that I think on it, instead there was admiration.

"Again you do well, mademoiselle," he said after a moment. "You have spirit."

I did not feel as though I had much spirit. In fact, I felt limp all over, especially when I realized that now I must go to stay at la Soeur Bourgeoys's.

"What of Madame Moitié?" Kateri asked. "Have you forgotten her, Hélène? We can take her there first rather than to la Soeur Bourgeoys's, can we not, Papa?"

I was so distressed that I did not answer. I just swallowed very hard and nodded. How could Armand have married? Why had there been no letter?

We continued down what the man said was Rue Saint-Paul, which I scarcely saw, for now my eyes were filled with tears. I blinked and blinked to force them back, and I could barely see Minette, who happily walked ahead of me on her lead. Kateri still held my other hand and now and again gave it a squeeze.

We stopped at a house, the door of which was open to let in the breeze. Even from where I stood, I could hear the sound of laughter and smell food. My stomach betrayed me and my mouth watered more than my eyes had.

The man and Séraphin stayed outside with the cart while we went in. I think of myself as a brave person, but beneath my skirts my legs were unsteady. Perhaps *ma tante* would throw me out.

Monsieur Aubry was speaking to an exceedingly short, plump woman. Her mouth dropped open in surprise, she wiped her hands on her apron, and she pushed her way through the crowd of men who stood between the two of us.

She kissed me on both cheeks, embraced me, and then held me away from her so that she could take a long look. "Hélène St. Onge. I never expected to see any of my husband's family here. *Une fille à marier*, is it? Ha! I wager there is quite a story for you to tell. But for now you need hot soup in your belly and a quiet night's sleep. And look, you have a little cat. A little cat is always welcome here as long as she is a good mouser. Is she a good mouser, *ma chère nièce*?"

I vow she said all of that in an endless flood.

I thanked Monsieur Aubry while my belongings were carried in and up the narrow staircase to the second floor.

"It is nothing, mademoiselle," he said with a wide smile. "Kateri and I will sleep well knowing you are safe here. I will send word to Madame Laurent of your whereabouts. *Bonne nuit*, mademoiselle."

"*Bonne nuit*, Monsieur Aubry. *Bonne nuit*, Kateri," I answered. Standing in the doorway, I watched them walk back to the cart. Monsieur Aubry was whistling. He seemed so much happier here, and so did Kateri, but then they had come home.

Tante Barbe was talking again. She called to a serving girl to bring food to the second floor. She bustled me up to a small room, told me I must eat, wash my hands and face, change into my night-dress, say my prayers and climb under the quilts. I should sleep well, she said, since this bed had a new mattress stuffed with cattail fluff.

That is how I came to be here in this warm bed under the roof of *ma* Tante Barbe.

le 4 octobre 1666

This morning Tante Barbe refused to wake me early, saying that I had needed to rest. I slept late. The sun was well up in the sky when she brought up a tray of food for me. There was cheese and fresh bread, a boiled egg and, unbelievably, a pot of chocolate. For Minette there was a bowl of milk and a piece of codfish. I felt my throat tighten at such kindness.

Tante Barbe patted my hand. "It is all behind you now, *ma chère*. Later, when you feel as though you can, you will tell me how it is that you have come here on your own." Then she hurried off, calling orders to the girl who helps her.

I admit that I feel guilty just lying here, but not so guilty that I could not have a second cup of chocolate.

ce même soir

I have had the talk with Tante Barbe. I wept and so did she. It is strange how dreadful it feels to cry, and yet how good it feels if you can share that unhappiness with someone else.

"You are now a *fille à marier*, Hélène, and so it is your duty to the King to wed here. You need not marry just anyone, though. Besides, you are too young still. Take your time. Make a good choice. I see you have common sense, but a successful marriage is made of more than common sense. Until then, you will stay here with me. I can always use another pair of willing hands." With a sniff she added, "I will arrange it with this Monsieur Deschamps. He may not like it, but he must understand that you are still a *fille à marier* no matter where you live."

I was learning that Tante Barbe loves to talk.

She looked at me in a very serious way and asked, "You have lived all your life with only your father. What household skills do you have?"

I mumbled something about being able to cook and milk cows and how I could dust extremely well.

She laughed. "A wife needs to have many skills, Hélène. I will help prepare you for the lucky man who will some day be your husband. Your papa made a good beginning, but this is New France."

Tomorrow we will begin. Since I left *Le Cadeau*, so many changes have taken place in my life. Only here can I admit how difficult and sometimes hopeless it all has seemed. Now, though, I feel as though my world may stay the same for a little while. At least I hope and pray that it will.

le 5 octobre 1666

I am tired, but content. I can see, though, that it will be a rare event for me to again write in this diary during the day. The morning begins slowly here at Tante Barbe's house. It certainly does not take long to reach a furious pace. I will write at night once I am in bed. Tante Barbe does not care in the least if I write in bed. She says that if I spill the ink I must wash the quilt myself. It seems a fair proposal to me.

There are only a few legal taverns in Montréal, Tante Barbe has told me. There are other places that sell strong drink such as brandy to the men, but her house is not one of them.

"None of that for me," she explained. "Ha! The fighting it causes! I have the two rooms upstairs that I let for ten *sols* a night, and I serve good food and weak beer. If the men bring their own wine or brandy to go with it, such is life."

I am to help with each part of the running of the house. No job is too lowly, Tante Barbe said. "You see, Hélène, each thing you learn to do properly here is something you will need to know when you have your own home. You will have an honest wage for what you do here, as well. Not so much as my other girl, Bernadette, since you live here and take your meals. You will begin at forty *sols* a week and when your skills grow, so will your wages."

I protested with embarrassment that she need not pay me.

She shook her head firmly. I was not an indentured servant or a slave, but her niece, and in a manner, her apprentice. "To be paid is only fair," she said. "That is the first lesson you have learned today, Hélène. Always be fair."

Apprentice. I had never thought for a minute that I might become anyone's apprentice. How exciting. The fact that I began my apprenticeship carrying a load of dirty linen from the rooms upstairs did not dull that excitement a bit. Each of those two rooms has four beds in it and last night the house was full.

I carried the linens through the kitchen and out to the yard behind the inn. As I stepped through the open doorway, I noticed the musket that leaned against the frame.

"It was my husband Jules's, and now it is mine," explained Tante Barbe. "Can you shoot, Hélène? No? Then you will learn in time."

A girl stood in the yard, her hands on her hips.

"This is my niece, Hélène, Bernadette," Tante Barbe went on. "She lives here now, and she has a great desire to learn how to wash linens."

We added more wood to the fire on which a large

pot of water was already boiling. I was to place the sheets in the pot without burning myself. This I did. Then lye soap chips were added to the pot. There was a paddle with which I could stir, and shift, and move the linens. In time, all the dirt would come out. Then one by one I would lift the sheets from the pot, again without burning myself, and they would be rinsed. Then we would hang them on a line. The fresh air would dry them and the bright sunshine would bleach them. For very bad stains the cloth might need to be soaked in sour milk for a week or so first. These linens were not so dirty, having been on the beds for only three weeks.

We paused for a moment and it gave me time to look around. Two cows stood near a small barn at the back of the yard, eating hay. There was a large kitchen garden. The beans, carrots and herbs had been picked, but there were still squashes, cabbages and pumpkins. Chickens, and a cross-looking rooster with a very fine tail scratched in the dirt. Minette considered the chickens for a second, but she is a good cat. She also hates being pecked.

"There is another pot here for the rinsing," Bernadette said. "The men took the cart and every bucket and jar that we have, and went to the river for water yesterday. At least we need not worry about that."

I offered to help do it next time.

Tante Barbe and Bernadette glanced at each other.

"No you will not, Hélène," ma tante said firmly. "You may walk about town to the shops, or to church, in safety during the day, but you will never, never go to the river alone. Has no one told you that we are at war here? It is far safer since the soldiers arrived last year. Still, no woman may go outside the palisade unless she is with an armed man, or unless she is armed herself."

I feel very safe here in my room. There is a rumble of low talk and laughter from downstairs. The men who have come to eat, or to simply sit and have some spruce beer and smoke their clay pipes, are all armed. There are soldiers downstairs too, soldiers who would know how to defend this place. I had forgotten the war with the Iroquois. Now I cannot stop thinking about it. When I think of learning to shoot it makes me feel very strange inside, but I suppose it is simply just another skill that a woman here must have.

le 8 octobre 1666

Séraphin has come to the house! Tante Barbe took him on as an *engagé*, saying that she needs the help of a strong young man.

"I thought to go west," Séraphin told me in the kitchen. "There is a party of coureurs de bois leaving next week to trade with the Indians, but perhaps this is wiser."

Another visitor came as well while I was chopping cabbage, and I went to the common room to receive him. He introduced himself. It was Armand Lecôté. I could not speak to him at first. I just stood there while he babbled, making excuse after excuse for himself.

Finally he said, "You hate me. I see that, and perhaps I deserve your disdain. I could not be certain that your sister had her dowry, and then the opportunity came for me to marry my dear Berthe. Surely you understand how a good dowry enhances a woman's prospects here, particularly amongst such as we Lecôtés."

I understood that, yes, I said. I also understood that courtesy in the form of a letter to Catherine had no meaning at all. Was that another tradition important to the Lecôtés? Then I went back to the kitchen where Tante Barbe had set Séraphin to work carrying in wood.

I took no pleasure at all in my outburst, for I had seen that it meant little to Armand.

le 10 octobre 1666

Today was Sunday, and so we went to mass. It was crowded, for this parish of Notre Dame is the only one in Montréal. The prayers and hymns were the same as those I have always heard in the church at home in Reignac. The behaviour of the people was not.

One old woman had brought a little white kid into the church. For some reason she had it wrapped in a blanket. It bleated during the singing. I believe it was too warm.

There was whispering, and laughter, and people wandered in and out. By the time the priest began to give his sermon, it was so noisy that he had to nearly shout to be heard. The people behind us were not listening anyway. I turned around once and saw that some were drinking what smelled like wine. One man raised his cup to me!

It made prayer rather difficult.

On the way back to the house Tante Barbe said, "Montréal can be a rough place for a young woman, Hélène. There are many good people here, though. It is hard to be poor. You have to be rough and strong to survive, and if their manners are not those of the court, then such is life."

She is correct, I suppose, but it will take me a while to become accustomed to Sundays. Still, the old woman's kid was a dear thing, although it stank horribly.

le 11 octobre 1666

Work. It never ends. If it is not one task then it is another, and some of them are very strange.

Like all good Catholics, we abstain from meat on the days we must, and do not serve it to our clients. Instead there might be fish soup or pie, salt eels or cod. Today I learned of another creature that some people eat, since it swims like a fish. Muskrat. They look a bit like rats, with their yellow teeth and long hairless tails, and so at first I had doubts.

A coureur de bois had brought six muskrats to the house. He made an agreement with Tante Barbe. He would trade the muskrats for a bed for the night and his dinner. Tante Barbe sometimes does such things, since there is a shortage of coins here in New France.

"Coins, Hélène — a *sol*, an *écu*, even a single *denier* — cash in one's hand is best. I admit that I am not above accepting even the Spanish coins that the officials despise." Under her breath she added, "The foolish men." Then she went on cheerily, "For today, the muskrats will suffice."

Here is where the work began. The coureur showed me how to skin the muskrats. We would have the meat, and he would keep the furs for trading, since Tante Barbe did not care to scrape and tan them.

It was bloody and messy, but I did manage to

skin one of them fairly well.

"Excellent!" he said. "You would do well in the bush, mademoiselle! I myself will remove the musk glands so the meat does not take on a very bad taste. See them here under the tail and elsewhere." He went on that I would not like that at all. Was he not kind to spare me this task? he laughed. I am finding that coureurs de bois usually say exactly what they think. They are very audacious.

Tante Barbe showed me how to cut off the heads and tails, and then quarter the carcasses. When I began to toss the heads, tails and feet into the big crock we eventually empty into the midden, she stopped me.

"Throw away the tails and feet, Hélène, but not the heads. They are the best part." How she laughed at my face. It is my fate to make everyone laugh.

I sliced onions and crushed garlic. We slowly fried them, then the muskrat pieces, and finally the heads in lard. It smelled good enough, but I did not particularly care for those little heads with their long, yellow teeth.

Tante Barbe served our coureur first, carrying in his meal in an *écuelle* and holding tight to its two handles. Then we served the other men who wanted muskrat. I took a small piece. Tante Barbe and the coureur kept the heads for themselves and left them until last.

"Are you certain you do not want to try one, Hélène?" she asked mischievously. I was certain.

They ate the meat from the heads, they ate the tongues, and then they cracked open the skulls, scooped out the brains and ate those as well. I may try it myself some time, but not soon.

le 12 octobre 1666

Minette wandered today. I am ashamed to say so, for I have always taken good care of her, but I realize now that she must have been gone for a long while. I could not find her to give her a bowl of milk when Bernadette finished milking. I was so worried. Then Minette suddenly walked in, with burrs in her fur.

"She is a cat, Hélène," Tante Barbe said gently when I said that I would keep Minette tied or locked in my room. "Cats love to wander."

I admit she was purring quite happily, even when I brushed the burrs from her coat. It would not be kind to tie Minette. She would hate that and I want her to be happy here. Look how far I have wandered, and I am not even a cat.

le 14 octobre 1666

A horrible thing has happened. To me it is horrible, although Tante Barbe says that any other girl would have leapt at the opportunity. With more than a little pride in her voice, she did add that I am not just any other girl.

Here is the horrible thing. Monsieur Deschamps has made a proposal of marriage to me.

He came to the house and asked if he might speak with me in private, so into the kitchen we went. This did not please him. Tante Barbe sent out Séraphin and Bernadette, and then she sat near the fire, her knitting in her hands, listening to every word. She did not need to listen very hard since Monsieur Deschamps spoke very loudly. He could have whispered, and the words still would have burned into my memory the same way that they did.

"I too am not above the law, and so I must wed. I am a wealthy man, mademoiselle," he said quickly. And then he asked for my hand in marriage. Perhaps his haste in speaking was because I sat there with my mouth hanging open. "My prospects are excellent, I have a fine house, two servants, a slave, and the services of the *engagé* who works for me in my shop. And I have a small library. I recall from the ship how you admire books. My income from my business as a merchant is more than good.

"All I require to make my life complete is a wife whose breeding will complement my own. I do not want just any wife, however. The girls who came across on our ship are decent enough, I suppose, but there is no unwed girl in Montréal at the moment who has your lineage."

It sounded as though he were discussing a horse. The urge to neigh was powerful. Lineage, indeed! It amounted to nothing, I said. Then I protested that I was too young.

"Nonsense," Monsieur Deschamps said with impatience. "Girls far younger than you marry. This is New France, mademoiselle. Remember your duty to the King."

Then he sat down and leaned back in his chair, the most comfortable one in the room, I may add, with a satisfied expression upon his face.

I mumbled that I was honoured, but that I must decline.

He looked extremely surprised at my refusal.

I stood and took a deep breath. I cannot believe I did it, but I said to him, "I do regret this, Monsieur Deschamps. I have a duty to His Majesty, yes, but I also have a duty to myself."

"I suppose you refer to love. Love has little or nothing to do with marriage, mademoiselle. Who has filled your head with such drivel?" He had the good sense not to glance at Tante Barbe. "Marriage is a business arrangement of the most delicate sort. Once the contract is drawn up and we are wed, you will be more than happy in your new home."

He babbled on about how I must think about it.

Would I prefer a life of work wed to a poor habitant, or the one he could give me? Keeping some miserable hovel, working beside my husband in the fields? He could not see that vile sort of existence for me, it seemed.

I refused him again, this time very firmly, and bid him *bonjour*. I turned to the table where I had been chopping onions and turnips to add to the eels that were simmering in a pot over the fire. It is a wonder that I did not chop off my fingers as well, so disturbed was I. The sound of his shoes on the floor as he left was an angry one.

How could the man see the habitants in such a light? How could Monsieur Deschamps think that a marriage did not need affection? Not at first, of course, here especially, where it is so necessary to marry for the sake of the country, but at least there must be some respect or mutual liking.

"Bien!" said Tante Barbe cheerfully. "He may seem like quite a catch, but he is a liar. Deschamps is like so many of the other minor nobles here, Hélène. He does not pay his debts and he is even keeping a tavern. Illegally. Ha! Yes, you may look surprised, but they just turn their eyes from it all. Privilege speaks here, *ma chère*.

"Deschamps is wrong," she went on. "Most make a marriage without affection, and hope that affection comes. Sometimes it does, and sometimes it does not. Such is life. Others feel differently. You will decide this for yourself, Hélène, when the time is right."

I can wait, I thought to myself. I can wait.

le 15 octobre 1666

Minette has begun to bring me gifts. She hunts ceaselessly, creeping about behind the house. Sometimes she eats the birds or mice she kills. Sometimes she saves them for me. If she lays these offerings at my feet I can praise her and then toss them out. This I do not mind. I do wish she would not now and again set them on my pillow.

A *potage* of peas and salt pork for supper tonight. The common room was full.

le 16 octobre 1666

Séraphin has brought in the last of the vegetables and stored them away in the cold room. They will keep there until ice can be cut once the river freezes. He has begun to turn over the soil in the garden with a pickaxe.

Tante Barbe has another piece of land outside the town. It is long and narrow, running right to the river as all the farms do. She has hired a man who owns a team of oxen to plough it, and Séraphin will assist him.

I made Séraphin a poultice of soothing herbs for his hands tonight. His palms are tough but he still has blisters.

"There will be no more storms at sea for me, mademoiselle!" he vowed. "A few blisters is a small price to pay. I do miss the ship a little, though, at times."

He went on to tell me that it was pleasant that there were no rats here to plague him when he slept. Madame Moitié did not beat him with a rope if she was displeased with his work, either.

Of course she does not, I exclaimed.

"Some do!" he confided, and told me of a boy he saw being flogged today when he went out for water. They say he did not bring in one of his master's pigs from the woods. "One pig short, and there he was!"

One pig short, indeed. Those who employ an *engagé* may have their rights under the law, but the sort of man who would beat a boy for the sake of a pig is *un cochon* himself.

le 19 octobre 1666

Monsieur Aubry and Kateri came here today. He brought a sack of black walnuts that he picked in the forest. At Kateri's heels was a large brown dog. This, I learned, is Ourson. Monsieur Aubry asked

Tante Barbe if Kateri and her dog might stay here, since he would be gone some weeks. He would journey to the Mohawk village of his wife's family.

"Kateri could remain at the shop," he explained, "but I prefer that she not be alone. She and your niece will enjoy each other's company. I will give you money for her room and meals, madame."

There was to be none of that, Tante Barbe told him. Bernadette had recently left to marry. Servant girls sometimes do rather hastily if they receive a proposal, so we were very short-handed. If Kateri was willing to help me with the work here, it would suffice.

I immediately offered to share my chamber with Kateri, and she was quite happy to accept the company. That decided, we sat in the common room while Monsieur Aubry drank a cup of beer before he went on his way. Tante Barbe began to leave but he stopped her.

"Madame, with your permission, there is something I wish to ask your niece."

"I would be careful what I asked her if I were you, Monsieur Aubry. Yes, though, you have my permission," warned Tante Barbe. Insisting we would prefer privacy, she hurried Kateri upstairs.

Kateri kissed her father good-bye.

"I will see you when you return, Papa. Be brave," she said mysteriously. "You as well, Hélène." Then she followed Tante Barbe out of the common room. I had not the least idea what she meant.

Monsieur Aubry cleared his throat and took a deep breath. Just then a group of men came into the house, filling the room with their laughter and noisy conversation.

"Mademoiselle," Monsieur Aubry said quietly as one of the men called out for him to join them. He only shook his head. They shouted that he must speak louder, that they could not hear him. "Mademoiselle," Monsieur Aubry began once more, but then a gust of wind rattled the door, causing us both to startle. "Do you think it may snow, mademoiselle?" he asked quickly.

I believed it might, I told him. It was so strong it might even blow him to the Mohawk village.

He had a little smile on his lips as he agreed that, perhaps, it would. Then he walked to the door and pulled it open. Flakes of snow were falling outside, and he decided then that he must quickly set out.

I wished him a safe journey, but still he hesitated.

"Mademoiselle," he said in a low voice, "when I return, there is something I wish to discuss with you." He glanced at the men who were now comfortably seated by the fire, calling for beer. "In greater privacy," he said with a small laugh.

In greater privacy, I agreed.

He gave a short bow, and then he was away. I

peeked out the door to watch him striding down the street through the snow. He was whistling again.

"Enough! Enough!" shouted Tante Barbe as she came down the stairs with Kateri behind her. The men, though, had quieted once Séraphin had started serving them.

I will put out my candle now and go to sleep. I think I can do this safely. Ourson is at Kateri's feet and Minette is on my pillow above my head. They seem to hate each other. There was a great deal of hissing and growling at first, but such is the way of cats and dogs.

Kateri seemed confused when I told her that her father had only wished to ask my opinion of the weather, but Tante Barbe did not. "He had to begin somewhere," she laughed. "Given the winters here, it is as good a place as any."

I am curious as to what Monsieur Aubry wishes to discuss with me. Certainly it is not the weather. There is an old saying about cats and curiosity, but it is nonsense, as Minette would say if she could only talk.

le 22 octobre 1666

Word came. Marie with the mole beside her mouth, and Marie with the missing front tooth, are to be married next Tuesday morning. Not a Monday this time, since that is the feast day of Saints Crispin and Crispinian, both the patrons of shoemakers. The priests do not perform marriages on feast days.

That leaves Marie who never speaks. How will she say yes or no to a suitor if she never speaks?

It also leaves me, I suppose. I get a strange feeling inside when I think of that.

le 25 octobre 1666

It was extremely cold last night and today the wind is blowing hard. I have never felt such a cold as I have since I came to New France. Kateri says I will become used to it. I am taking only a few more minutes in bed to write, before we prepare ourselves to leap up and dress in the cold. We were warm under the quilts last night and it is warm enough downstairs. Fortunately this house has two fireplaces, one in the common room and one in the kitchen. Many houses have only one. When the common room is full, and it often is, it is comfortable.

But Tante Barbe calls.

ce soir

The day was filled with work. A dozen coureurs de bois arrived and all were calling for hot meals. That is why Tante Barbe called for us to help. The common room quickly took on the odours of pipe tobacco and unwashed men. Food interests them far more than washing and changing the clothing in which they have been living for weeks.

Monsieur Deschamps appeared shortly after. He stood at the doorway and held a lace-trimmed handkerchief over his nose for a moment. Then he saw me and in he came. I myself had to wait upon him and serve him the meal he ordered. It was a savoury *potage* of fish and wild rice and it smelled tempting.

Monsieur Deschamps finished his meal, sipped the wine he had brought for himself, and set his coins on the table. He had paid far too much and I told him so.

"Ah, Hélène," he said, boldly using my first name. "What remains is for you. Buy yourself a silver cross and some silk ribbon." He looked down at my simple wooden cross and sniffed. "My intended must have the finest of everything."

I took what he owed for the meal, leaving the other coins, and said that I did not need a new cross. Mine suited me quite well, *merci*.

He sighed dramatically. "Hélène, have you been thinking of my proposal?"

I actually had now and again, mostly when I dumped a chamber pot, but I did not say that, although I was greatly tempted.

le 26 octobre 1666

The weddings were joyful events. Marie with the missing front tooth is now Madame Drouillard, and Marie with the mole beside her mouth is Madame Ouellette.

They will both leave Montréal tomorrow to live with their husbands on their respective farms down the river. They were so excited. For the rest of this winter there will be the inside work and the feeding of the farm animals, but when spring comes both of them will work beside their husbands clearing the land and planting the crops. I am not certain I could do that. Papa often said that one does what one must.

I did not stay for the dancing, however, once I saw that Monsieur Deschamps was there.

le 2 novembre 1666

Today was All Souls Day, and so Tante Barbe and I went to mass. It was a special mass, one we had said for Catherine's soul and for the souls of Maman and Papa. On this day last year Catherine, Papa and I had a mass said for Maman. Catherine and I had planned to do the same for Maman and Papa today. But so much has changed. This morning I knelt in a church an ocean away from home and prayed for my entire family. I am all that is left.

I felt sad and empty all day, no matter how Séraphin and Kateri tried to cheer me. But the house was busy, and so, slowly, my misery slipped away. Papa used to say that work cures many things. Can it cure a heart that has been torn in two? Perhaps in time.

le 5 novembre 1666

It snowed hard in the night. Although it was windy and cold, I thought the snow made everything look clean and beautiful. Tante Barbe laughed at that.

"Winters here are not like winters in France," Tante Barbe said. "And now we must do the laundry inside and use the drying racks. Ha! You may not think snow is so beautiful when it is up to your waist, Hélène."

I have been told many times about the winters in New France. It will be colder than one can imagine, the storms are dreadful, and the snow piles up in huge drifts. But it was agreeable enough this morning when Kateri and I went out to feed the chickens and to milk.

"Both of you wear your *sabots*." Tante Barbe could not resist giving more advice before we left the kitchen. "Maple wood is better in this snow than leather. Your *chaussons*, too. Felt over your stockings will keep them from wearing."

The cows awaited us. They are *Canadienne* cows, which is the breed of cow that is raised here. Brune and Noisette were named for the colour of their big brown eyes. They are good cows whose ancestors came from Normandy. They do not kick over the bucket and spill the milk.

They stood quietly while I milked Brune. Both cows had the cowpox on their udders, so I was very gentle. It was rather enjoyable to sit on the little stool, my head leaning against the cow's flank. My hair smelled of cow afterwards, but there are worse smells.

Minette waited patiently for her bowl of milk still warm from Brune. This she drank, and then washed her face daintily with a paw. When Kateri came in from feeding the chickens, she dusted off her hands and then milked Noisette. Then we carried the pails of milk across the yard to the kitchen. We stepped very carefully, for with *sabots* it is quite slippery in the snow.

The kitchen is far more pleasant than the barn. Tante Barbe has many copper pots and other iron pots with little feet. There is a spit for roasting meat. The plates, porringers and cups are on shelves. Tante Barbe uses only glazed earthenware in the common room. The good pewter service is kept for special occasions.

We baked, as we do every day. White flour is too

expensive, so we use a mixture of wheat, rye and barley flours. It is quite good, especially with fresh butter. While I churned, Kateri used the long paddle to take the round bread from the bake oven. Then she put in more unbaked loaves.

The soldiers who come here enjoy it, since this bread is so much better than what they must eat when out in the bush. Those loaves are called soldiers' bread and they are coarse and heavy. There are many soldiers in Montréal now that the weather is turning cold. Soon there will be even more, since they do not all stay out in the forest during the winter.

le 8 novembre 1666

We are both skinny creatures, Kateri and I, but together our weight has stretched out the ropes on the bed. Last night was quite unpleasant with us rolling together into the middle of the mattress, and with all the hissing and growling. That was Minette and Ourson hissing and growling, not us.

We tightened the ropes before retiring tonight. Then we swept the floor, sprinkled dried herbs on the boards to give the room a sweet smell, and climbed into bed.

Kateri has her finger weaving. I have my diary. I have decided to try to learn a few words in Mohawk. I will set them down so that I can read and practise them. It is a difficult language.

Here are the words for tonight. I will simply write them as they sound. *Kwe*. It means hello. *Onen* means good-bye, and it sounds precisely as it looks. Last, *Kateri*, which is pronounced just as I have written it. Kateri means Catherine. Strangely, that makes me feel both happy and melancholy at the same time. My sister is gone, but my friend is here with me.

le 11 novembre 1666

Poor Kateri. She has the cowpox. It is only a mild affliction, but it will still take a few weeks for her to heal. Tante Barbe says I must nurse her through the fever, and keep her from scratching the blisters on her hands. There is no doctor here, only some very good midwives, the nuns at *Hôtel-Dieu*, and a surgeon. What Tante Barbe had to say about the surgeon's lack of skill was shocking.

Kateri does miss her father, who has been gone longer than we thought he would be. So I read to her, tell her stories, and we make plans for the days of Christmas.

le 13 novembre 1666

I had a nightmare last night. It was all tangled together with Catherine's death and Kateri's illness.

I cannot bear to lose anyone I love again. Kateri is much better, but seeing her in the bed, so unwell, brought back the sad memories of Catherine's passing.

le 23 novembre 1666

An unspeakable thing. A party of men cutting wood outside the town were attacked by Indians. They tried to defend themselves, but they were far outnumbered. Two men were killed and their scalps taken.

Kateri's fever is gone and she feels better. I want to ask her about the scalpings, but I cannot.

le 24 novembre 1666

Today Kateri and I walked to a merchant's shop up the street. It was snowing heavily, but there was no wind, and so the flakes settled on our capes and whitened them. When we stopped at the door of the shop we were covered in snow, so we shook ourselves off before stepping inside.

Other people were there. One woman was fingering a roll of cloth, her back to us. A man was in deep conversation with the proprietor, who held a shiny new musket. I simply wanted ink powder, paper, sealing wax and, for Tante Barbe, a packet of needles. I had a list of things for the house that I was to give to the proprietor: candles, soap, flour, lard. Those he would have delivered, being too much for us to carry, especially in such a snowstorm.

You can buy or trade for nearly anything here. Thread, scissors, fabric, smoked pork or smoked eels, wine, clothing and all sorts of tools were set out on the shelves or kept in the storeroom at the back of the shop. It all comes from France. There was not much difficulty in finding what I wanted, but it was interesting to wander about and examine the goods.

The door opened and a man came in, bringing with him a rush of cold air.

"We have arrived from Québec, monsieur," he announced. "There was no trouble. Your goods are all here. The others are carrying them up from the common."

I knew then that he was a coureur de bois.

"You have managed to keep *les sauvages* from taking your scalp yet again, *mon ami*," said the proprietor. *"Bien!"*

I glanced at Kateri, but she did not return the look. She was staring at the floor. I quickly paid for the goods, put them in my bag and gave the proprietor Tante Barbe's list. I slipped my arm through Kateri's and we began to leave.

"They say your papa has gone to the Mohawks once more," the coureur de bois called out to Kateri's back. He wiped his dripping nose upon his sleeve. "That is dangerous business these days. He must not be too fond of his own hair."

I could feel Kateri trembling as we left the shop. She was not crying, but she was very close.

"It reminds him of my maman," Kateri said, and I could hear the sadness in her voice. "That is why he returns to the village. I go too sometimes. Maman's family is there, my grandmother and grandfather and everyone else." She stopped in the street, fumbled about in her pocket, and pulled out her handkerchief. She gave her eyes a wipe and blew her nose.

We walked back in silence. If he misses her so very much, then perhaps Monsieur Aubry will never be able to forget his wife.

le 25 novembre 1666

It is the feast of Sainte Catherine. My sister was in my thoughts all day. How she enjoyed this day back at *Le Cadeau*, the mass in the old church at Reignac, a brisk walk home with Papa, the added attention the servants paid her. Catherine was at her happiest during such times.

I must keep those happy memories of her always, and try to forget the rest. I do understand how Monsieur Aubry's wife remains in his mind. I wish that

I could talk to him of this, but I cannot. It is something I must bear alone.

le 28 novembre 1666

Monsieur Aubry's shop is not far from us. Kateri, Tante Barbe and I took a walk past it after mass.

"There it is," said Kateri with great pride. "This is Papa's shop and our home."

Some buildings here are of wood, and some are of stone. Monsieur Aubry's is made of wood and stone. A sign hung above the door announcing his profession: *Monsieur Aubry Armurier*. Below that was the image of a musket, for many people would not have been able to read the words. It is most unusual for such a sign to have words at all, and I suspect that Monsieur Aubry is very proud of his shop.

"It is locked, Hélène, or I would take you inside," Kateri went on.

I could wait until another time, I assured her. I said it was a lovely house. And it was. The shutters, closed tightly in Monsieur Aubry's absence, were painted a dark green, as was the door. There were two storeys. It was not nearly as large as some of the other houses owned by the wealthy merchants on this street, but it had an elegant appearance.

Tante Barbe thought that Monsieur Aubry was wise to purchase this building. She said so as we set out for home. She could recall when it was very shabby. Monsieur Charbonneau, the shoemaker, had it then, but Monsieur Aubry had turned it into a good business and a comfortable home for himself and for Kateri.

Later I asked Tante Barbe what became of Monsieur Charbonneau, thinking that I would hear yet another story of disease or murder. He, though, hating the cold beyond all reason, merely went back to France. On a night like this, with the wind howling, I can almost agree with him.

le 2 decembre 1666

I have discovered that I cannot spin very well. The Intendant, Monsieur Talon, encourages the raising of sheep. Sheep mean lambs and mutton and, of course, wool. Tante Barbe has a spinning wheel. Although she does not have time for such things, she said I must try to learn. The yarn I spin is full of lumps. Still, it is something to do in the evenings before we retire.

le 3 decembre 1666

More blisters on Séraphin's hands. He and other *engagés* have worked these last few days with the soldiers to replace a section of the palisade.

"They say it rots endlessly, mademoiselle," he

told me as I mixed yet another poultice. "We would not be nearly as safe here without a strong palisade for protection." He paused since Kateri was in the kitchen with us. "Against bears and snakes and such," he finished.

How Kateri laughed at that.

le 4 decembre 1666

We go to bed early and rise early. The coureurs de bois and other men who come here to spend a bit of time at the end of their day work hard, and are often up before dawn. No habitants come. They are asleep inside their houses before even we retire for the night. The life of a farmer here is very difficult.

So are the lives of the women they marry.

le 5 decembre 1666

Tante Barbe sent Kateri and me to the hospital today with fresh bread and a pot of soup.

"It is the least I can do for Mademoiselle Mance," she said. "How good she was to my dear husband Jules when he died."

Jeanne Mance is yet another kind woman who thinks only of others. She came to this island with the first group of people from France. They say Montréal might have failed had it not been for her. She began the hospital of *Hôtel-Dieu* here, and her first patients were men wounded in battle with the Iroquois.

Montréal is not like La Rochelle or even Reignac. It is like some small stronghold under constant siege, but there is la Soeur Bourgeoys's school, and the hospital, and all the houses. I cannot imagine what it must have been like when Mademoiselle Mance stepped foot here more than twenty years ago.

She is far braver than I could ever be.

le 6 decembre 1666

My hand is shaking as I write this.

Kateri and I had a long talk as we sat in the kitchen this afternoon spinning. Rather, Kateri was spinning and I was creating knots in the wool. I suspected that she wished to share what had so distressed her in the shop.

"There have been only a few marriages here between Indian women and the Canadians or French," she began slowly. "I am not certain why. Most Mohawk women do not want to marry them. Papa says there are too many differences in the way the French see things."

She looked carefully at me to see if I was taking offence. I was not.

"My father loved my mother very much, Hélène.

He is French, and yet there is a part of him that became Mohawk. He had his shop here, but he also lived amongst the Mohawks for three years before he wed my maman, you know. I was born there. When Maman died, we left the village. Sometimes he needs to return."

We were both quiet for a while as we thought of what she had said. When she spoke next, her words were filled with pain.

They were wed in the Mohawk way, she told me. The priest did not marry them. Her maman was baptized after Kateri was born, but she died before the priest could marry them.

"Here they say that there was no marriage at all, that it was for convenience only and that I am *batârde*." I could barely make out her next words. Her father told her she must ignore the gossips, that they had no idea what they were saying and that it was a lie. "I try, Hélène," she whispered finally, "but it hurts me."

I held her as she wept. Now she sleeps. I do not know what to think. All my life Papa told me about the sacredness of marriage. The ways of the Mohawks are very different from ours, far more different than anyone has wished to tell me. Surely they hold marriage to be sacred in their own manner.

Papa said that I should not pass judgment until I knew everything there was to know, and many times one should not judge at all. I only know that Monsieur Aubry loved his wife, and he loves his daughter. She is his true daughter, and if I hear anyone use that foul word to her, she who seems so defenceless, they must deal with me, her loyal friend.

le 7 decembre 1666

Saint Nicholas's feast. It makes me lonely for Papa and Catherine and Louise. I have tried all day to think of other things.

Séraphin, as always, was a help. "Come watch the game," he begged me and Kateri, and so we walked with him to the gate. He carried an odd looking stick with a small pocket of sinew at one end.

There on the common were at least two dozen men, some from Montréal, some Indians. They raced across the field, hooting and screaming, bashing each other, tripping one another, slipping in the snow, and through it all, laughing aloud.

"What is it?" I asked. "Why are they doing this?"

"Is it not wonderful?" exclaimed Kateri. "Join them, Séraphin!" Then to me, "It is *Teh hon tsi kwaks eks* in Mohawk."

"The Jesuits call it lacrosse," Séraphin shouted over his shoulder as he joined the battle.

It took us an hour to clean his wounds that

evening. He did not seem to feel the pain at all, even when he spat out a broken tooth. Lacrosse is not for me. I have all of my teeth and I intend to keep them.

le 9 decembre 1666

A heavy, wet snow. Tante Barbe says they sometimes rake the snow off the roofs, there is so much. I do not want that job.

le 12 decembre 1666

Our room is so cold tonight, that both Kateri and I wore two pairs of stockings to

I begin again. When both a dog and cat sleep in your bed and the cat decides to jump on the dog, it is not necessarily wise to be balancing an ink bottle upon your lap at that moment. There will be extra washing tomorrow, meaning more work, but how it made Kateri laugh!

le 14 decembre 1666

Monsieur Aubry has returned to Montréal. Kateri and I were working in the common room, wiping tables, when he opened the door and walked in. She was overjoyed to see her father and, naturally, all work stopped.

"Bonjour, mademoiselle," he said to me and he made a little bow.

I answered and gave him a brief curtsy. Ourson was leaping about, his tail wagging crazily, but Minette sat near my feet in a dignified manner as though to say, "Foolish dog."

I must say it gave me such pleasure to see Monsieur Aubry. His cheeks were red with the cold and his *capote* crusty with snow. Although he was flushed and looked tired, there was a happiness in his expression that I had not seen before. Perhaps his visit to the Mohawks had done him good.

He set down his musket and pack, and pulled off his mittens and cap. He unwound his sash and slipped off his *capote*.

"Are you hungry, Papa?" Kateri asked him. "We have been cooking and baking all day. Hélène's *tourtières* are delicious, for she is a good cook. She used the best of salt pork and some venison. Her crust is much more flaky than mine, Papa."

I blushed dreadfully at all this. I loathe blushing nearly as much as I hate to cry. Both are so hard to control.

"It sounds excellent, but I think I will decline," said Monsieur Aubry. "I truly have no appetite."

We had no other customers for the moment. Kateri sat down close to her father while he gave her news. Ourson curled at their feet, and for a moment the scene caused me pain. They looked so content-ed and so much a family.

"Come join us, mademoiselle," Monsieur Aubry said gently.

"Yes, join them, Hélène," Tante Barbe ordered. She added that I should walk with Monsieur Aubry and Kateri when they returned home, to put some colour in my cheeks.

She bustled through the room and out again. I vow that is the only way to describe the way she walks. One moment the room is empty, and then it is filled with the presence of Tante Barbe.

I thought my cheeks could not have held more colour, but I removed my apron and sat down across from them while Monsieur Aubry answered Ka-teri's unasked questions.

Their family was well. It surprised me at first to hear this come from his lips, but of course, it was his family also. There was no sickness in the village yet this winter. Greetings were sent to Kateri.

Monsieur Aubry told Kateri to fetch her things, for it was time to go.

"Would you accompany us, mademoiselle?" he asked me when she returned.

I said I would be pleased.

"I have a gift for you, mademoiselle, and one for you, Kateri," he went on as he pulled something from his pack. "Please do not protest that it is not proper to accept a gift from me. This is something you need. Few French or even Canadienne girls wear them, but you are sensible and will immediately see why you should."

"Papa!" cried Kateri. "New *bottes sauvages*! I will show you how to put them on, Hélène."

Monsieur Aubry wore the same things on his feet. They were the winter shoes of the Indians, made of heavy greased leather, he explained. The leather at the top was elk skin. It wrapped around the leg and was laced shut in a criss-cross manner.

"Your feet will be warm and dry," said Tante Barbe, who had come into the common room carrying a covered crock.

She decided to walk with us, although it had nothing to do with propriety; Monsieur Aubry was a gentleman. She just wanted to take some soup to Madame Pitou who was still so lonely since her husband died. She called an order to Séraphin to take charge.

"Oui, madame," he said cheerily. Then to a coureur whose cup was empty, "They say you have come from the west, monsieur. Let me pour you another and you shall tell me tales of adventure. For a coin, that is."

Wrapped snugly in heavy cloaks, we females, a dog and a cat made quite a procession as we walked down Rue Saint-Paul with Monsieur Aubry. The day was cold but clear, the sun sparkled on the snow, and suddenly I felt a lightness in my heart that I had not felt before.

At the shop, Tante Barbe left us to continue to Madame Pitou's house.

Monsieur Aubry tried to pay her for the food Kateri had eaten these last weeks, but Tante Barbe waved away the notion. Then her eyes sparkled. "I suffer for fashion, but I hate cold, wet feet. I would take a pair of those *bottes sauvages* when you are able to get them, though." The idea satisfied Monsieur Aubry. He is a proud man and the idea of charity in any form displeases him. I had learned that.

She made sure Monsieur Aubry would escort me back, then, before either he or I could say a word, she hurried away.

He unlocked the door and we stepped inside. It seemed colder here, but that is always the way with houses in winter when they are left empty. He lit a fire with a striker and flint, blowing carefully on the little spark that caught in the charcloth. Then he added tinder. It would not take long to heat, we were assured.

With Ourson following them, Monsieur Aubry and Kateri went to the back of the shop to the kitchen, to begin a second fire. Minette gave a little token hiss as Ourson passed her.

Alone now, I examined the room. This was the

work area of a craftsman. Monsieur Aubry's tools were laid out neatly. There was a forge with its bellows, and a workbench. He is a gunsmith and has the skill to make good muskets, but he does repairs as well. It was clean and orderly.

Minette jumped up on the workbench and stretched out. She is a haughty cat.

"She is at home here, mademoiselle."

I turned and faced Monsieur Aubry. He scrubbed at his face with his hands and suddenly looked so weary. When I protested that I could easily walk back alone, he would not hear of it.

"I will make you something hot to drink for when you return, Papa, if you wish," Kateri offered.

"No, *ma chère*," he answered. "My head and back ache. Perhaps I have a cold."

We walked back in companionable silence, although he coughed now and again.

My bed seems rather empty with only Minette and me in it. I know, though, that Kateri's place is with her father. I will say a prayer for Monsieur Aubry before I sleep. He did not look well at all when he bid me *adieu*.

le 18 decembre 1666

Tante Barbe, who always enjoys a gathering, is planning a *fête* for Christmas day with a special meal, and she says she will invite Monsieur Aubry and Kateri to share it with us. After I milk, tomorrow, I will walk to the shop and invite them.

le 19 decembre 1666

They have accepted.

le 20 decembre 1666

I happened to have Minette on my lap this morning. When she rolled onto her back, as she loves to have her stomach scratched, I gasped at what I saw. Her nipples stuck out and were very pink. The fur around them had receded.

Tante Barbe leaned over, looked and nodded. "Well, well. *Bien.* Our Minette is *enceinte.* In six weeks or so she will have kittens."

I nodded silently. My little Minette, who is still a kitten to me, was to be a mother. I had tried to keep her inside during the cold weather, and she had only been out once in the last weeks. I fear I thought aloud. How did it ever happen? I wondered.

"The same way it always happens, Hélène," said Tante Barbe, who laughed until she cried.

Later, when I was up here in my room, she came to me and sat on the edge of the bed.

"Hélène, I know you had only your papa, and he may not have spoken to you of the responsibilities of marriage," she began carefully.

Papa had been very clear on that matter, I assured her. He was a scholar and a philosopher, after all, even if he had studied only dragonflies. I had known for a very long while about marriage and babies and, indeed, about where kittens came from. She smiled at that.

"As for the kittens and other things, I suspected as much, but I had to be certain," Tante Barbe said. *"Ma chère,* what a joy it is to have you here with me."

How that pleases me.

le 21 decembre 1666

Tante Barbe and I will go to Angels' Mass at midnight on Christmas eve. When I told Kateri about the kittens, I invited her to come along as well. We could meet outside the church, I suggested.

She said she would come, and then asked me if she could have a kitten. Almost as an afterthought, she asked Monsieur Aubry if that would be all right. She was pleased when we both said yes.

Then, before I could stop and reconsider, I

extended the invitation to Monsieur Aubry.

"My shop has been closed since I returned, and I have done little work. I have a touch of illness, mademoiselle, but if I am well, then, *oui*, I will attend mass with you," he said tiredly.

Perhaps he has made his peace with the church. Perhaps it is only that he wished to please me. It does not matter. He is coming. I will say a prayer for his quick recovery.

I did not like the way he looked at all.

le 25 decembre 1666

It is Christmas morning, just after mass. Neither Monsieur Aubry nor Kateri came to the church last night. Perhaps he has worsened. I will go to the gun shop and see later today. I feel so uneasy.

le 31 janvier 1667

So many days have passed since I last opened this diary, that at first I wondered if I would even remember how to write. Much has happened, but as Papa said often, it is best to begin a story at its beginning.

I walked to the gun shop on Christmas afternoon. It was so, so bitterly cold and snowing hard. I left Minette at home, since I was carrying a basket of *tourtière*s, some fresh bread and a little pot of butter.

If I had three hands I might have brought Minette, but I do not, and so she remained by the fire.

Most people were at home. A man riding a horse passed by me. He must have been a wealthy man, since there are few horses here. A few couples, their faces hidden by hoods and scarves, leaned into the wind as they walked.

I knocked at the door to the gun shop. There was no answer and so I walked inside the shop. No one was there and the fire was dead. I called out for Monsieur Aubry and then for Kateri. There was no sound at first, but then she ran into the shop from the kitchen.

"Oh, Hélène," she cried. "I thank *le bon Dieu* that you have come. Papa is so sick." She said that he fainted last night, and that she dared not leave him.

We hurried to the kitchen. Monsieur Aubry, covered by a quilt, lay on a mattress that Kateri had managed to get under him. She said she could not carry him to his bed. The fire in this room was still burning well.

I tossed my cloak to the floor and knelt beside him. I touched his forehead. He was hot with fever and his shirt was soaked through. He moaned and turned his head to the side. Strands of his hair were stuck to his cheek. There was water in a basin and a cloth on the floor next to him. I gently pushed aside the sweat-dampened hair so that I could bathe his face. Then I saw it.

Kateri cried out. She began to moan and rock back and forth. "It cannot be. It cannot be. No, Papa. No."

Monsieur Aubry had the smallpox. Many illnesses look the same, and it is easy to confuse them, but I nursed Papa when he had the smallpox. I will never forget the look of the pox.

"I will run for Séraphin," Kateri said. "He can carry Papa to *Hôtel-Dieu*. He must be taken to the hospital."

I grabbed at her arm and stopped her. I was certain they would not permit Monsieur Aubry to enter the hospital, I told her. If Kateri went out, then others might catch the smallpox from her. We must bolt the door, stay inside here, and nurse him ourselves.

Tante Barbe came later that afternoon to see why I had not returned. I told her the horrible news through the open window.

"It breaks my heart," she said, "but I cannot come in." The pain in her voice was terrible to hear. She said she would bring us anything we needed, and would pray for Monsieur Aubry. Then she wiped her eyes and whispered, "I will pray for Kateri and for you, Hélène, that you do not get the smallpox yourselves."

I had stayed with Papa and not caught the pox

from him. I only prayed that Kateri would not become ill with it. There was no sense in her leaving, since she had already been exposed to the illness. I prayed every moment that Monsieur Aubry would live. I had nursed my papa, but he had died in spite of all I had done.

The days and nights passed slowly. Kateri and I took turns staying with her father, bathing his face and body, urging him to take sips of water. He was covered with the pox blisters, and I had to tie mittens over his hands so that he did not claw himself. He was so ill.

Tante Barbe came many times each day. Sometimes she had food for us. Other times she had words of encouragement or news. Each day one of the priests stood outside the shop and prayed. One night Tante Barbe sang to us. The sound of *"Un Flambeau, Jeanette, Isabelle"* brought tears to my eyes. How could she have known that it is my favourite Christmas song?

Séraphin came when he could, to stand in the street and tell Kateri or me news of the town. I sometimes barely heard him, so worried was I for Monsieur Aubry, but his kindness moved me.

"I went with the soldiers to cut ice from the river where it is shallow," he said. "There is not much yet, but they say it will be thick in time."

He told me that Marie with the mole beside her

mouth, that is, Madame Ouellette, came into the town with her husband a few days ago. They took a meal at the house and paid with a bag of corn. Madame Ouellette said that she would remember us all in her prayers.

It seemed that coureurs had arrived from Québec, though it was late in the season. There was no trouble with the Indians on the way, but the coureurs were making trouble now. They wandered the streets singing and calling out. Other men, some of the young nobles here who could afford to do so, urged them on with brandy and even joined them, dressed as Indians.

"Madame says they are hopeless scoundrels and should be turned out of town," said Séraphin.

His voice faded and then stopped, for it was clear I barely listened. At last he whispered, "Mademoiselle."

I looked up.

"Will he live?"

I told him I did not know.

Le 1 janvier, the feast of the circumcision of the baby Jesus, and *le 6 janvier*, the feast of the Epiphany, both passed by uncelebrated by Kateri and me. There were people in the street walking to mass, but they stayed well away from the gun shop.

One afternoon Monsieur Aubry opened his eyes.

His fever had lessened the night before, and now when I carefully set my hand on his forehead, it was quite cool. Kateri was asleep on the floor nearby, with Ourson at her side.

Monsieur Aubry raised his hands and looked at the mittens that still covered them. When he saw the blisters that were all over his arms, he closed his eyes so that he would not have to face the horror of it.

They will heal, I told him. He was getting better, the blisters would dry up, the scabs would fall off, and he would grow stronger each day. I had soup for him. He must take a little.

He turned his face away from me.

Kateri woke then and wept happily that her father was beginning to recover. Tears came to my own eyes.

Monsieur Aubry regained his health. Slowly his appetite grew, and each day he spent a bit more time on his feet. When he began to grumble about how he needed to be out of doors, how behind he was in his work, I knew he was truly better.

I made plans to return home. Wearing fresh garments, Kateri and I burned the bedding and the clothing we had worn while caring for her father. We cleansed the shop and kitchen by burning dried lavender and cedar chips that Tante Barbe brought us. The smallpox was gone from this house. I thanked *le bon Dieu* that no one else in Montréal had caught it. I could at last leave.

Séraphin came to fetch me. He said it was good to see me without a window frame between us.

I kissed Kateri good-bye, and then I had only to make my farewell to Monsieur Aubry. I found him alone in the kitchen, staring at the reflection of his face in a small mirror. His cheeks were covered in scabs. Where the scabs had dried and fallen off, he was deeply scarred.

I vow that I truly intended to simply say *adieu*, but instead something much different came out of my mouth. Months ago, he had wished to ask me something, I reminded him. We have privacy, I added.

Monsieur Aubry regarded me with the saddest expression.

"What does it matter now?" he muttered into the mirror. He faced me then, and went on. "I thought to ask that I might court you, to spend time with you in a proper manner so that we might come to know each other better. That has all changed."

I could not say a word at first. Monsieur Aubry's face reddened and he apologized for his forwardness.

I told him then that Monsieur Deschamps had made an offer of marriage to me. Monsieur Aubry became quite pale at that.

"You accepted?" he asked me.

Not at all, I told him. I did not care for Monsieur Deschamps or his beaver hat, and besides, I was too young to marry.

Monsieur Aubry said he agreed. He sounded very relieved. "That is why I wished to ask for time," he said. "We could simply have spent time pleasantly together and come to know each other." Then he faltered. "But I cannot possibly afflict you with the monster I have become," he said.

But that would leave me with a *truly* monstrous offer of marriage, that of the beaver-hatted Monsieur Deschamps, I told him. Could he abandon me to such a thing? Then I said yes, I agreed to spend time with him pleasantly, so that we might get to know each other. "So far it has not been too pleasant," I teased him.

He smiled crookedly. He said they would have let him die here. No one else would even have come into the house, so immense is the fear of smallpox. "Kateri would not have left me," he said, "but she had no idea what to do. You did. I owe you my life, mademoiselle. Anything I can ever do for you to repay that debt, I will do."

I daringly suggested a walk about the town when he had time. He smiled again, more happily this time.

I am in my own bed once more, lying here between clean sheets. Minette, with her enormous belly, is at my side. Although it is never a good idea to bathe too often, especially in winter, I washed my hair and my entire body when I returned home. I stank of the sickroom. Even Séraphin, who is not particular about such things, wrinkled his nose at me.

I wish Monsieur Aubry did not have to bear those scars, but there is nothing to be done about it. Papa always said that *le bon Dieu* would never send us more trials than we could abide. I have always wondered about that. Perhaps it is true. I know one thing. I have lost everyone in my family, and I doubt that I could have dealt with the loss of Monsieur Aubry. He has scars on his face, but inside himself, where it matters, there are no scars at all.

It has occurred to me that for the first time I have written of this place as home. It does seem like home to me now. What a blessing.

Here are the Mohawk words for the day. *Friend* is *orye. I am happy* is *wakatshennonni.* Kateri has told me the word for smallpox. I will not write it here.

le 1 février 1667

It is the first day of the month. *Février* in Mohawk is *Enniska*, which means *lateness*.

There is a fierce snowstorm, and no one has come in today, so I have time to write here by the fire. How strange that such a small thing gives me such pleasure. The wind blows so hard that the shutters rattle and the cold is dreadful. Minette has ceased her wandering. Tante Barbe says her time is very near. She is, in fact, calling me from upstairs, so I must go to see what she wants.

ce soir

When I came into my room, for it was from my room that Tante Barbe had been calling, Minette was not asleep on my bed, where she sometimes is at this time of day. Tante Barbe had found her in my chest, for the lid has been open of late, and she was not alone. Five tiny kittens were there with her, nursing. One is black like Minette, two are orange, and two are grey. There are many orange, black or grey cats in Montréal. I wonder if I will ever be able to guess which of them is the papa of the dear kittens?

le 2 février 1667

The storm has ended. Monsieur Aubry arrived at our door today, towing Kateri on a *traine*, which is a sled they make here out of birch. The design is very clever. Its curved front ploughs through the snow, and a man can pull heavy loads on it. He himself wore snowshoes, large paddle-like objects that he had strapped on over his *bottes sauvages*. He told me to dress warmly and come with them.

When I asked him if he was certain he could pull such a weight, he said that the two of us did not amount to much at all.

"Enjoy the day," Tante Barbe called from the kitchen. And when Minette tried to follow us, "Ah me! Come, Minette. It is too cold for your paws. Your kittens need you. Come to see them when you return, Kateri."

The day was more frigid than anything I have ever felt. Kateri sat behind me, and we were bundled in cloaks and blankets so that only our faces showed. Ourson trotted alongside us. He was wearing boots of leather that protected his paws.

Up and down the streets we went. There were many people out walking in spite of the cold. Other *traines* slid over the snow behind them. The business in Montréal rarely stops even for the weather, I have come to understand. I did not know most of the people, but I recognized some. I could see la Soeur Bourgeoys and her friend Mademoiselle Mance just leaving the school.

Then I saw Monsieur Deschamps. A servant preceded him, sweeping snow out of the way to make his master's passage easier. You would think he was the King himself for the fuss that was being made. It was too fine a day for thoughts like that, however. I made myself very small inside my wrappings. He still saw me.

"Bonjour, Mademoiselle St. Onge," he said with formality. He swept off his hat, made a low bow and set it back onto his wig. He had a new wig, I noticed. It was very long and curly, and would have made an excellent muff.

I answered his greeting. He said *bonjour* to Monsieur Aubry and Kateri as well. I was not at all surprised that not a word came from them. This did not stop Monsieur Deschamps at all. He said he had heard a rumour of Monsieur Aubry's smallpox. "The scars are remarkable, are they not? Do not despair, monsieur, some girl with poor eyesight and a liking for *les sauvages* will probably not mind so much." Then he bid me *adieu*, and said he would call on me soon. Off he went at the heels of the sweeping servant.

When we returned to the inn Kateri and Monsieur Aubry came inside to warm themselves. Kateri went into the kitchen to see the kittens where they and Minette had a nest near the fire. While she was gone, I assured Monsieur Aubry that Monsieur Deschamps's words meant nothing to me at all. I despise cruelty and rudeness. He had shown both. Perhaps I would dump the contents of a chamber pot on his head after all, if he came to call.

Monsieur Aubry laughed at that. "I will make certain not to warn him," he promised.

I have said the rosary tonight in hopes that I will be able to control my temper when I next see Monsieur Deschamps. Perhaps I should say it twice.

le 3 février 1667

Only Kateri came this evening, her father remaining at home to work. It seemed strange, and I realized then how fond I was of his company.

Unfortunately, Monsieur Deschamps also arrived at the inn, and in spite of the fact that the room was filled with men, pressed me openly for an answer. With elaborate courtesy I asked him to please cease this. I had no wish to marry him. I turned away from him, fighting my anger.

He said nothing for a moment. Then, "This is about Aubry, is it not? Yes. I see it is."

I turned then. His face grew ashen and then very red. I do not wish to set down here the rude things he said about Monsieur Aubry. It seems that those who spend time with the Mohawks, wed their women and, worse, have children by them, do not belong in the same society as Monsieur Deschamps.

"He is less than an animal, Hélène. He lives like one. Would you choose that fate for yourself? I think not." Insisting that I will come to my senses, out he went.

I walked slowly to my room and wept for the cruel things Monsieur Deschamps had said about my friends. I thanked *le bon Dieu* that Kateri had been in the kitchen with Tante Barbe and had not heard. The words hurt me as much as if they had been spoken about myself.

Then I became cross with myself for letting Monsieur Deschamps's words touch me at all. Minette batted my face with her paw as if to say, "Do not cry, Hélène," and it comforted me.

When I came back downstairs, Tante Barbe and Kateri were in the common room.

Tante Barbe did not ask me what had happened. She only said that one of the men should open the shutters. The room was very smoky and their pipes were making her dear niece's eyes red.

le 4 février 1667

Monsieur Aubry asked Tante Barbe if he might borrow Séraphin for some hours.

Séraphin told her that he had worked hard this morning, mucking out the cowshed and chopping wood, so Tante Barbe agreed. They left with Monsieur Aubry carrying his musket and a big sack, and Séraphin carrying a net and a pole.

How I wished to go with them. I am able to safely walk the streets during the day, but the world beyond the palisade is too dangerous.

When they returned Monsieur Aubry asked to borrow Séraphin again this afternoon, before it grew too dark.

"We cut holes in the ice and used the pole to stretch out a net," Séraphin explained excitedly. "We weighed it down with rocks. There will be fresh fish for supper tonight."

There was. When they returned Monsieur Aubry emptied a sack of whitefish and small pike onto the kitchen table. Kateri and I gutted and scaled them. They made an excellent dinner fried in lard.

Food is all I think of some days.

le 9 février 1667

There has been an attack. I heard about it in the morning, and at that time learned that a man and his wife were both killed. It was not until this afternoon that I discovered their names.

Hers was Ouellette.

It was Marie with the mole beside her mouth, and her husband. It was not the Mohawks, they said, but Indians passing through. One could tell by the arrows that were left in the bodies. The feathers used for the fletching were those of another tribe.

I have cried and cried. I did not know her well. Marie came all the way from France to make a life here. To live. Not to die in the wilderness.

le 10 février 1667

When he came with Kateri to the house this evening, Monsieur Aubry was carrying a bundle.

He had the *bottes sauvages* he had promised Tante Barbe. She immediately put them on. Then he said he had something for me as well. Something important.

"Ha! Something important, is it?" Tante Barbe answered. "Come help me a moment in the kitchen, Kateri." Oh, how she conspires to leave us alone together. I despair of it, and thank her in my prayers all at the same time.

Monsieur Aubry set the bundle down on the table and unwrapped it. Inside were a flintlock pistol, a leather belt and two flasks.

"I made this pistol myself, and so it is of the highest quality. If you would buckle the belt around your waist, I will show you how to hang both the pistol and the powder flask from it. This flask contains ball. It goes as so. There. Now you are armed."

How heavy it all felt hanging there. I was armed, I remarked, but I had no idea of how to shoot. I did not think I could. Monsieur Aubry stopped smiling then, and said he would teach me. He wanted my assurance that I would learn to use the pistol accurately, and that if I ever had occasion to be outside the palisade, which I must not, that I would wear it. "You saved my life," he said. "This weapon may save yours some day." He paused then and spoke in a quiet voice. "At worst it could keep you from falling into the hands of Indians."

I agreed to his plan and so did Tante Barbe. For me it was a pensive evening. Monsieur Aubry assured me that no harm would ever come to me from the warriors of Kateri's village. He has told them of me. Nevertheless, there are other Mohawks. Could I bring myself to shoot one of them? Could I ever use the pistol on myself, and commit a sin for which I would be forever damned, for surely that is what he meant? I hope I never learn the truth of that.

le 12 février 1667

Monsieur Aubry has told me that they had the smallpox at his wife's village. He heard the news from a Mohawk who came here to trade. The sickness was not too severe, though, and Monsieur Aubry's and Kateri's family was spared.

He added that he had heard that some in Montréal are celebrating, and some are even praying that the smallpox takes all the Mohawks.

I now know how to load and prime the pistol. Peace will never come to New France as long as there is so much hatred, I fear.

The dear little kittens have begun to open their eyes. At least that is something good and happy.

le 14 février 1667

I shall sleep well tonight, since I spent a long while in the fresh, cold air today. I went outside the palisade for the first time since I arrived. Monsieur Aubry took me out on his *traine* to the common. Soldiers were there, standing guard while men were drawing water from where the river does not freeze.

He set a large gourd on a rock. I loaded the pistol and fired. I loaded the pistol and fired again. I did this ten times until my hands and arms were shaking.

"Madame la Courge eludes you, mademoiselle," called out one of the soldiers, but it was in good fun.

On the way back Monsieur Aubry said that I must ignore them. Only practice will perfect my aim, and I will practise under his supervision as often as possible.

le 15 février 1667

There is time for a few sentences before I go down to the kitchen this morning.

A wet snow fell in the night. Today it is not so cold. Children played outside, and rolled the snow into balls to build snow people, just as children do in France. I wonder if the children at Kateri's village do the same thing?

Snow in Mohawk is *oniehte*.

le 16 février 1667

There is sickness in the town. Many people have bad colds. There is a feverish ailment of the lungs and there are some cases of measles. They say that the surgeon bled them all to no effect. Three people died in the night, but mercifully, there is no smallpox.

le 17 février 1667

Even in winter, the men fell trees and cut wood. It is so cold here that it takes a great amount of wood to keep a room warm. The farmers burn the wood from the trees they clear from their land. What a life they are living. It takes a year, they say, to clear just one *arpent* of land, and that only if the man works diligently.

Tante Barbe pays a man to cut our wood, and she

prefers ash, oak or other hardwoods, since they give the most heat. She does not care much for cedar or spruce or fir. They burn too quickly. But they do have another use.

"We need to make beer, Hélène. I would rather use rice, but there is none to spare, so it will be spruce. There is nothing like fresh spruce beer."

I have not been impressed with the odour of the old spruce beer we have been serving, so perhaps she is correct.

We chopped up spruce tips and boiled them in water. Sometimes Tante Barbe uses fir or cedar. The spruce was then taken out. Molasses should have been added, but there is none, so we used a bit of sugar. Then the mixture boiled again. Séraphin ladled off the scum. When Tante Barbe said it had boiled long enough, it was left to cool. This is spruce essence.

We then boiled more water, poured it into the spruce essence, and added a large cup of yeast. I mixed it very well. Then we put it into barrels so that it could ferment for three days. We will continue to add water as this happens.

le 18 février 1667

Séraphin tapped pierced bungs into the barrels so that the beer may be vented. Otherwise the barrels would explode. What a thought!

We will taste it in three or four days. Tante Barbe says it will be delicious, and I am in for the delight of my life. I believe her . . . but then, she likes muskrat heads.

le 19 février 1667

Monsieur Aubry has agreed to take on Séraphin as an apprentice. Séraphin will continue to work for Tante Barbe, but will spend half of the day at Monsieur Aubry's shop. Monsieur Aubry will teach him to shoot as well.

There are no guilds here, but Séraphin will learn the craft just as Monsieur Aubry did in France. There is little respect for a common labourer, but as a gunsmith he will have a good living. He will learn blacksmithing and woodworking at first. Then later he must be able to carve attractive designs, and do finishing work on the metal. In time he will be a master craftsman.

I have taken on the far more difficult task of teaching Séraphin to read and write. He must be able to do this if he is ever to have a business of his own. We began tonight with his first name.

What a chance this is for him.

le 20 février 1667

The fresh spruce beer is hideous in both taste and smell. We have so much! It is fortunate that so many of the men who come to stay here have a taste for it. As she always does, Tante Barbe hung several small spruce branches on the door to tell passers-by that fresh spruce beer is available here. I think she should hang an entire tree. Then the beer will disappear more quickly.

Monsieur Aubry enjoys a cup of spruce beer. He had one this evening as we sat near the fire. Kateri leaned over a table with Séraphin while he practised writing his name and a few simple words. I suspect that Séraphin would rather have a game of cards or *tric-trac*.

Monsieur Aubry talked about his work while I listened. He had undertaken several new repairs on muskets, and he had nearly finished making a fine firearm for Intendant Talon. He and the Intendant had gone shooting when Monsieur Talon was in Montréal, so that Talon might try one of Monsieur Aubry's muskets. I felt a puff of cold air as the door opened, but I did not look up, for people constantly come in and out.

"I will be well paid for that job," said Monsieur Aubry. "Talon does not mind paying for the sort of musket he wants. He is a respectable man. Not like some." He was looking toward the door with a slight frown on his face. I looked too. There was Monsieur Deschamps.

He asked politely if he might have a word with me. "Alone," he added.

I declined. I had given him my answer, I reminded him.

"Your answer was not acceptable to me, Hélène," Monsieur Deschamps said, less sweetly. "There is only one response I will accept, and that is yes. I would like to hear that from you so that we may marry before I leave for Québec next week." And then he added that although I had agreed to become a *fille à marier*, months had passed without me agreeing to marry.

Again I told him no, that he did not want such as me for his wife. After all, I do not see well at all and I like Indians. How his eyes widened at that!

Monsieur Aubry stood. "You have your answer, Deschamps. Leave her be or you will regret it."

"I should challenge you, Aubry," hissed Monsieur Deschamps. "Though I doubt you possess a rapier."

I reminded Monsieur Deschamps that duelling was against the laws in France and, I suspected, here. I suggested that Monsieur Aubry ask Intendant Talon himself the next time they went shooting together. I feared for a moment that Monsieur Deschamps's eyes would pop from his head and roll across the floor. If they did, Minette would have them in a flash.

Monsieur Deschamps said huffily that he would discuss this with me another time. Again he added, "Alone."

He would not, said Monsieur Aubry quietly, for he doubted I had given Monsieur Deschamps permission to call me by my first name. "For a man of your breeding that is quite a *faux pas*," he reminded him.

"You are wrong on the first count, but absolutely correct on the second, monsieur. *Pardonnez-moi*, Mademoiselle St. Onge. Until later, then." Out he swept.

When Monsieur Aubry sat down, I said to him that although I did not care at all for Monsieur Deschamps being so familiar, I would not mind if *he* called me Hélène. If he wished to. In private.

It seemed he did wish to, but only if I would call him Jean. "In private," he added.

I realized how much listening to that argument had taken out of me. Catherine used to think that having men fight a duel over her would be most romantic. She was wrong. Again and again I found my thoughts drifting back to the distasteful scene, but I tried not to let Monsieur Deschamps's visit spoil the evening.

When Jean and Kateri left, he paused a moment, his head tilted to one side.

"Put Deschamps from your mind," he said firmly. "He is of no importance. And I thank you for the most enjoyable evening, Hélène. You have a talent for rising above unpleasantness that cheers me."

His words cheered me as well.

le 22 février 1667

My mind is at rest now after today's news, but how anxious I was at first. More and more soldiers of the Carignan-Salières Regiment are being brought back from Fort St.-Louis. When I learned that these men are all unwell, I felt a moment of terror, thinking that perhaps it might be the smallpox. It is not. However, they are all quite ill, and those who may not live have been taken to *Hôtel-Dieu*.

Jean brought a haunch of venison. Tomorrow is Ash Wednesday and Lent begins. There will be no meat for us for a long while, so we enjoyed it greatly.

le 24 février 1667

Tonight Jean told Tante Barbe that I managed to nick the gourd today with a pistol ball. "Her aim is improving," he said.

I admit that I felt a certain pride that I was beginning to master the pistol. However, the sense of satisfaction went further. Although I would be unable to say it aloud, it filled me with pride that I had pleased Jean. Still, I pray that the gourd is the only thing I must ever shoot.

le 7 mars 1667

There will never be a duel, for which I am very grateful, but I cannot help but feel sorrow at the reason why. Monsieur Deschamps is dead. His party was set upon as they travelled to Québec, we have heard. All were killed.

"We will pray for him," said Tante Barbe as she crossed herself. "He was a pompous fool, but he did not deserve that end."

No one does.

le 10 mars 1667

How I long for something fresh and green. Still, we eat better than many people do. Tante Barbe's husbands left her a prosperous widow, and she makes a good living from her boarders. Certainly we have none of the things that the wealthy have. There are no sugared almonds or brandied fruit. But the room at the back of the kitchen is filled with tubs of cabbages, beets, carrots and turnips. Barrels of salt pork and eels line the walls, and there are bags of dried peas for soup. Garlic and onions hang in bunches. The smell of dried herbs, savory, fennel, basil, sage, thyme, meets my nose every time I go in.

le 12 mars 1667

Another terrible storm. This morning we could barely open the front door! And until it is cleared away to make paths, with the snow so deep, it is so hard to walk if you must go outside.

Beyond the palisade and the town, life is surely much harder for the people. I wonder how Marie with the missing front tooth is faring? I pray that she and her husband will be safe.

le 15 mars 1667

Tante Barbe and I took pots of hot cabbage soup to Mademoiselle Mance at the hospital. The men there are a pitiful sight. It is scurvy, but no one knows what causes it. Their mouths are bleeding, their arms, legs and bellies are terribly swollen, and they cannot walk. Mademoiselle Mance said that she has seen it many times before, and almost always in the winter. With good food the men slowly will recover.

le 17 mars 1667

All of us here at the house have colds. How wretched I feel, but a running nose and cough is no excuse to stay in bed.

le 19 mars 1667

Tante Barbe said this morning that I kept her awake in the night with my endless coughing. I was feverish when she put her hand on my forehead, and so she dosed me with comfrey tea and ordered me to my bed, where I slept for much of the afternoon. Once I awoke, it seemed so strange to lie here, while downstairs the life of the house went on. I did not care for it at all, but it is impossible to disregard Tante Barbe's commands and her tea.

Jean, I need not write, remained in the common room this evening, but Kateri came up to spend a little time with me. She says she will come to help Tante Barbe tomorrow.

le 20 mars 1667

Restlessness and guilt drove me from my bed this morning. I had no fever and although I still cough, I do feel well enough. This I vowed to Tante Barbe. Jean did not seem pleased at first this evening when he learned I had worked all day as I always do.

"You know, yourself," he said, "to leave a sickbed too soon is foolishness."

I whispered to him that one more dose of that tea would have drowned me.

How he laughed.

le 25 mars 1667

When I woke this day I saw that, strangely, there had been a fog in the night. It froze upon the trees, turning them all silvery. It was so beautiful.

le 1 avril 1667

Jean says he can smell spring coming. Séraphin once said that he could smell land. It must be a wonderful thing to be so much a part of something that you can nearly see inside its mind. Perhaps a time will come when I am that closely bound to this place.

Until then, I content myself with the smell of the bread I baked today.

le 5 avril 1667

I would like to wash the floors in the kitchen and the common room. Sweeping is not good enough since the weather is suddenly milder, and the snow is melting. We bring in muddy water throughout the day and we track it into the kitchen. Straw might be spread to soak it up, but Tante Barbe said it would just be worse.

I wiped down the tables, washed crockery and then put on my cloak. We needed wool and some large needles for darning stockings. I also wished to buy some felt so that I could make another pair of *chaussons* to wear inside my *sabots*. My old *chaussons* are quite worn.

I walked carefully through the slush to the shop of Monsieur Salon. He has the best fabric, I have decided. More importantly, he is fair and pleasant. Naturally, I had to pass Jean's house.

Jean says that the sap has begun to run in the maple trees. The Mohawks make a sweet syrup with it. That would be a wonder to taste.

le 10 avril 1667

It is Easter Sunday. After mass Kateri chose a grey kitten and named it *Kanon'tinekens*, which means milkweed in Mohawk. What a long name for such a tiny creature.

le 11 avril 1667

This afternoon I hit the gourd. Bits of it flew everywhere.

"Excellent, mademoiselle," one of the soldiers

cheered. "*Madame la Courge*'s head makes a satisfying target, *non? Les sauvages* will flee you in fear."

I was sickened. I felt all the blood draining from my face. Jean and I did not speak as we walked back to Tante Barbe's house. At the door, just before he left, I began to confess to him that I could never kill another person. He put up his hand and stopped me.

"Do not say it, Hélène. I know that you would find the strength to do anything you had to."

He has more faith in me than I have in myself.

le 12 avril 1667

I have taken one of the quilts from my bed and I am still comfortable and warm, since the weather has changed. Yesterday there was ice on the river. This morning it is almost gone. I walked to the gate through a light drizzle to see for myself.

It was raining harder by the time I returned. I had left the shutters open in my room, and I found Minette sitting there watching the drops falling. She did not reach out to play with them as she once had in France. I did not feel any desire to take off my shoes and stockings and run through the puddles as I once had. It was not the cold, either.

"Are we both so much older?" I asked Minette. She did not answer.

le 13 avril 1667

Today was so mild that we threw open all the shutters to freshen the air in the rooms. Tante Barbe was seized with the need to clean everything, and so I tied a scarf over my hair and helped her. Moreover, we were able to do laundry outside again.

Jean brought something to the house tonight. With the fine weather, the forest across the river has begun to come alive once more. The wild cherries soon will be in bloom and all the trees have little buds. There are some wildflowers, and best of all, he said, the ferns are coming up in a few sheltered places where the sun warms the earth.

Jean, Séraphin and Kateri are precisely like Tante Barbe in that they will eat anything. I will not. Yet I must admit that I was tempted by the tiny ferns that Jean called *têtes de violon*. They are shaped like a fiddle's head, and were delicious served with butter, garlic and a little salt.

le 14 avril 1667

What happiness! Marie who never speaks has agreed to marry the widower, Monsieur Lespérance, who is a carpenter.

I would have liked to hear that acceptance myself.

He is much older than she, and has been married twice before. It is a relief to me that she will not have to live outside of the protection of the palisade. They will be married next week on Monday. Tante Barbe and I are invited. Sadly, I noticed that my best gown is no longer very presentable at all. I sponged the hem, but there are worn spots and a stain.

"Thrift is commendable, Hélène, but not when there are all those gowns and *chemises* packed away in Catherine's chest. Do not argue. Come let us see what may be done."

I protested that I was too short, that I was too thin, that such gowns did not suit me at all. It is interesting how Tante Barbe becomes so hard of hearing when she chooses to do so.

We unpacked the clothing and, in an instant, I was back in France folding these lovely garments. The faint smell of herbs, the odour of cloves, lavender, mint and thyme grown in our own garden, rose up like a ghost. I could almost see Catherine standing near me, her hands on her hips, her lovely brows drawn together in concentration. I felt my throat tighten horribly.

Tante Barbe, who as always, sees everything, began to bustle. It is her solution to many problems, and as always, it helped. She shook out a *chemise* that had lace at the cuffs, and then a skirt made of claret-coloured wool. It was soft and beautiful. There was a matching bodice with a straight neckline.

"This one to begin with," Tante Barbe decided. "Try it on."

When I expressed my doubts Tante Barbe said, "Hélène, you do not seem to realize that you have grown these last months. Not a great deal, but you are fuller here and here. I can easily take in the waistline of the skirt and put tucks in the bodice. You shall raise the hem yourself. Look in the mirror, silly girl."

Tante Barbe gave me a small hand mirror. Bit by bit I looked at myself, and finally agreed that, yes, it might do after all.

le 16 avril 1667

The weather remains fine, which is a delight after the long, harsh winter. The muddy streets are filled with people. Some have things to trade, such as cheeses they have made, or a few precious bags of dried berries. Some are venturing out to inspect the fields they will soon begin to plough, and some are simply out for the pleasure of it. There is a smell of animal droppings from the sheep and cows that are being driven out to the common.

Séraphin has turned over the soil in the kitchen garden. I will plant the peas tomorrow. Later there will be cucumbers, shallots and all the herbs we need for cooking as well as healing.

Jean says that there is wild chervil in the woods. He will take me there to pick some in time. It is a small thing, but how I look forward to it. Minette shall come too. I am becoming more like her each day, I have told her. I can nearly understand her desire to wander.

le 18 avril 1667

It is difficult for me to think, for I feel such happiness. Yet I believe I must begin with the happiness of another, and write about Marie's wedding. Perhaps it will bring me some calm.

I wore the claret gown to the church today, with my wooden cross and mourning ring as my only jewellery.

Marie and her husband exchanged their vows before all of us. At least I think she did. I could not hear a word Marie said. It was chilly and damp, the day again being rainy, and so I kept my cloak about my shoulders. Later, back at the home of the bride and groom, I could remove it.

Monsieur Lespérance's shop smelled of newly cut wood, since he makes furniture as well as working on houses. It did not take long for his home to become crowded, and for the rooms to become too warm. In spite of the light rain, men stood outside in the street making jokes about how old Monsieur Lespérance was, and how young was his bride.

"You look different tonight, Mademoiselle St. Onge. Whatever can it be?" Jean teased. "Is it that your hair is dressed in a new fashion?"

"It is such a lovely gown, Hélène," said Kateri loudly, for it was growing noisy. "You look like a bride yourself. Does she not, Papa?"

Later, when the rain stopped and the men came back into the house, Jean and I stood alone outside to take the air.

"The night is pleasant, is it not?" he asked me.

Most pleasant, I agreed, but it was not simply the clean air. It came to me how enjoyable it was to be with him, how content it made me feel.

"Hélène," he said suddenly, "we have spent time together each day. Would you consider my proposal of marriage? It has been my hope you would see that we could make a good life together. I am not so old, only thirty years." Seeing my wide eyes, he hurried on. "I will not press you. There is time for courtship. You need not even consider it courtship if you find that distressing. We may simply continue to see each other."

I paused and thought, I am a *fille à marier*, and this is why I am here. To consider a man's proposal is my duty, but it does not feel like a duty at all. I am not distressed, I assured him, and yes, I would consider his proposal. How happy I felt once I had said it.

The rain began again, this time a downpour, and so in we went.

"You asked her! I can tell by looking at you, Papa," Kateri cried. "What did you say, Hélène?"

"She is an intelligent girl," said Tante Barbe. "Of course she said yes."

I was an intelligent girl with a very pink face, I fear.

le 19 avril 1667

The first thing I thought of upon waking was that I had agreed to consider Jean's proposal. The memory flooded through me in a way nothing ever has. It was such a remarkable mix of happiness, nervousness and excitement, that I felt I must immediately

ce soir

There has been a scandal. Séraphin came shouting the news this morning, and so I quickly dressed and left writing until tonight.

There was no dancing at Marie's wedding. There would have been, but there was no space at all. That must have pleased the priests.

Instead, there was a charivari. Men stood outside the bedroom window of Marie and her husband until nearly dawn. Séraphin went out in the night, drawn by the noise, and saw it for himself.

He later told us that someone played a fiddle, and the men sang rude songs and threw pebbles against the shutters. "Finally, Monsieur Lespérance opened them, leaned out and tossed down some coins. What a sight he was!"

Back in France, I thought that the charivari was very amusing. What harm in the young men showing they thought that man far too old for his bride? Papa agreed, but Catherine never did. Certainly she was correct. Now I believe it is not quite so amusing as I once thought.

le 20 avril 1667

Good news and melancholy news. How it seems life is always made up of both. The melancholy is that Jean will set out to hunt tomorrow, very early, and he is taking Séraphin with him. I will miss them both, each in a different way, but I do enjoy the thought of the fresh meat it will give us for our table. The happy news, though, is that Kateri, her kitten, and Ourson are staying with us. What hissing and growling there is yet again!

Kateri is asleep next to me. It is much warmer sharing a bed, and she does not snore at all. If I were to wed Monsieur Aubry, Kateri would be my stepdaughter. How odd. That is far too complicated to think about at this hour, however.

le 21 avril 1667

Today Kateri and I took the other kittens to the people who had asked for them. An orange kitten went to Marie and her new husband, Monsieur Lespérance. A grey kitten went to the school, and an orange kitten to the sisters at the hospital. Tante Barbe and I will keep the black kitten. We have named her Sottise, for all the mischief she gets into.

Strange. She is just like Minette and loves to wander.

le 28 avril 1667

I fear the night will be a sleepless one, for I cannot find Minette or Sottise. Naturally, Tante Barbe says not to worry. Cats will be cats. Cats will wander. It will be hard to sleep tonight and writing is a comfort.

le 29 avril 1667

Sottise came home, I thank *le bon Dieu*. Minette has not. The weather grows colder and it is snowing heavily once more.

le 30 avril 1667

I walked the streets today through the snowstorm, calling for Minette. Kateri came with me. I know it is a childish thing. It is only a cat, some would say, but I have to find her. No amount of calling helped, and so we have returned home.

le 2 mai 1667

Where to begin? I feel foolish and relieved and, although it is difficult to say which emotion is the stronger, I thank *le Bon Dieu* for watching over us all.

This morning was cold, and although the skies were grey, the snow had stopped. I went out to search for Minette. I bless Tante Barbe, for she said nothing and I have truly been neglecting my work.

There was a dead mouse on the front doorsill of the house. The paw prints of a cat that were surely Minette's led off down the street.

So did the footprints of Kateri. Her *bottes sauvages* left a clear trail. She would have heard me weeping in the night. She knows how important Minette is to me.

I said nothing to Tante Barbe, for my thoughts were on what I must do. I paused then, and ran back up the stairs to my room. I loaded the pistol, buckled on the belt and hung the pistol at my waist.

It was very early, and so few people were about. I followed the prints to the open gate of the palisade. There is a little shelter there for the soldiers who stand guard. They were inside, and took no notice of me when I slipped out.

I despaired then, for the footprints led out onto the common and it had begun to snow again. The footprints would quickly disappear. I knew I should not venture out alone. How many times had Jean warned me of what might happen? If I was killed or taken, that would be one thing. But what of Kateri? With no further hesitation, I walked straight out of Montréal to search for her.

By the time I crossed the common and approached the river, the wind was blowing horribly, and the snow falling so hard that I could see little. The footprints were gone. I called and called for Kateri.

Faintly, above the wind, I heard her.

"Hélène," she cried. "I can see you. Do not move. I will come."

Then we were in each other's arms, both saying how foolish was the other for coming out into such danger. We turned in circles trying to see the town through the snow so that we might return, but everywhere was swirling white. If we misjudged, we might fall into the open water of the St. Lawrence and drown. It had happened to others. If we stayed here, we would freeze to death.

An Indian warrior came out of the storm. He was heavily armed and his face held no expression. My heart pounded hard as I began to step back. He said something in his own language. I had no idea what it was. He took a step towards us. It was then that I took the pistol in my hand and pointed it at him, my body between him and Kateri.

"Hélène, stop! Kateri! What are you two doing here?" It was Jean and he was furious. "Lower the pistol, Hélène. He is one of my companions from the village who has come here to trade." Behind Jean were other warriors. Séraphin stood with them, his red hair blowing from his cap. "He asks only why a white woman is out here when others hide like frightened rabbits within the walls. She is either very unwise or most fearless."

I felt my whole being sag as I let the pistol drop to my side. Jean's eyes were enraged.

I told him I did not know, that I would not ever let anyone harm Kateri. And that my Minette has been gone for days in this storm. Then anger crept into my words. "Can you not understand how hard it is to lose something dear to you?"

"I understand perfectly," Jean said in a quiet voice.

The warrior clearly knew Kateri. He said something to her. She replied. When he spoke again, I could hear laughter in his words. The other warriors smiled and elbowed each other.

"Do not repeat that," Jean said quickly to Kateri and ordered us both back to the town.

Montréal's palisade was a dark smudge off to the

left. We began to walk towards it when a voice called out behind us. There at the river, just reaching the shore, were five canoes. We watched them land, and then men and women began to get out.

"Bonjour, monsieur," a tall man called as he walked towards us. "What a time we have had of it. These women must get into the warmth of a building. It is a happy day for the men of Montréal, monsieur, for more *filles à marier* have arrived."

There they were, tired, frightened and excited all at the same time. They had been in Québec since the late fall, it seemed, but were here at last. I could see Madame Laurent fussing about. Soldiers ran from the palisade cheering, *"Vive le Roi! Vive les filles à marier!"* How it stirred the memories in my heart.

The Mohawks left us, going to their own encampment beside the palisade, and we walked back into the town. To my relief, Jean no longer seemed so cross, although he should have been, I suppose. He walked ahead of us with Séraphin, the two victorious hunters carrying the squirrels they had shot, talking to the tall man. Madame Laurent fussed and chattered as she led the girls through the gate.

"I know you will perish from curiosity if I do not tell you what was said, and I cannot have that," Kateri whispered, dropping back a little. She said the warriors suspected who I was, since Jean had described me to them many times. She paused, mischief dancing in her eyes. "They wished him luck."

When at last we returned to Tante Barbe's house, it was she who now was extremely cross.

"Hélène and Kateri, you foolish girls, you have disobeyed me, and I cannot think of what to do with you. Nothing perhaps, since I am so relieved to see you all in one piece. Confession? A long and horrible penance?" Perhaps she should send to France for two hair shirts, she cried. Only the sight of those fat squirrels calmed her a little. What a *potage* she would make with them! Séraphin would be a wonderful provider for some lucky girl. On she went, until she paused for breath and shook her head. "Ha! You need a husband, Hélène. Does she not, Monsieur Aubry?"

I admit I was not listening at all. All I could do was stare at Minette, who sat close to the fire, asleep. I mumbled something about how I would have to believe that cats would be cats.

It was not until later I realized that Jean had not answered Tante Barbe's question.

le 3 mai 1667

Jean says that the Iroquois plan to sue for peace at Québec, and a treaty will surely be signed. Tante Barbe and I prayed together this morning at mass to give thanks.

le 4 mai 1667

I have already crushed the end of my quill and, after
cutting it to a sharp point, dropped it twice. This
page is all blotted, so I have tried to calm myself
before I begin again.

Jean and Kateri came as always. We sat quietly
talking as Minette and the kittens played, Kateri
having brought *Kanon'tinekens* along. Kateri and
Séraphin had started a game of cards, when someone opened the door and walked in. It was the tall
man who had arrived with *les filles à marier* and
Madame Laurent.

He said breathlessly that he had been told this
was the home of Mademoiselle St. Onge. I said that
it was.

He handed me a packet, a letter from France.
"Madame," he went on, waggling his eyebrows and
flirting openly with Tante Barbe, "they say you have
the finest spruce beer in all of the town. I would
appreciate a cup."

"Ha!" sniffed Tante Barbe, but she could not keep
from smiling.

Once he sat drinking on the other side of the
room, and Tante Barbe had returned to her chair, I
broke the seal on the letter and began to read it
aloud. It was from Cousin Pierre. He was most distressed to have learned of Catherine's death, and

ashamed of how he had permitted Madeleine to treat us. Anne had made an excellent marriage to the Vicompte de Patisse, who had a charming brother, Jerome. As my guardian, Cousin Pierre had taken the liberty of beginning negotiations with this Jerome, and was willing to provide me with a good dowry so the family alliance would be strengthened further. I must return to France immediately.

The tall man overheard me telling Tante Barbe this news. He said he would be travelling back to Québec in a few weeks, and would be happy to take me if I could be ready. "One of the priests and Madame Laurent will be with us, so it will be quite proper," he added.

I thanked him. Then I looked at Jean, who was watching me in grave silence.

"I must go upstairs," I said to him.

He stood. "I understand, Hélène," he said softly and regretfully.

No, he did not, I told him. Would he please stay? It would not take me long to write an answer to my cousin. I would tell him I was sorry to ruin his arrangements, but that I had accepted a proposal of marriage from a fine man. By the time the letter reached France, I would be wed.

The expression on Jean's face said what words did not.

Séraphin and Kateri were so happy for us. Tante

Barbe kissed me again and again. The rest of the evening was filled with excitement as Jean and I made our plans. And the tall man who would carry my letter back to Cousin Pierre? Tante Barbe gave him another cup of beer at no charge.

le 5 mai 1667

A fierce thunderstorm woke me just after dawn. I opened the shutters of my room to see if any snow remained, and there it was. A rainbow. How it, and the thoughts of last evening, made me smile.

The house is stirring and, in a moment, I will get up and dress. I have taken off the mourning ring, and carefully put it away in my chest. Rest in peace, Papa and Catherine, I whispered as I did it. I know they would have approved.

Papa said once that a dragonfly is the perfect symbol of life, and indeed, of one's search for knowledge and understanding. When it is a nymph, it spends months in the darkness, deep under the water of a pond. Then one day it climbs a cattail stem and emerges into the air. Its back splits open. It is a great struggle, as life always is, but it prevails. Then it spreads its wings and soars into the sunshine of a new world. Today I believe that the door to a new world has opened for me.

Epilogue

❖

Hélène St. Onge wed Jean Aubry on August 18, 1667, having received permission to be married on a Thursday, which was the day she turned fifteen. Their marriage itself would have been enough cause for celebration, but there was another reason: a peace agreement had been reached between the Iroquois and French at Montréal the month before.

The wedding feast was the best Tante Barbe could create. There was dancing, good food, laughter and, since Jean was so well respected, no charivari. People talked about the celebration for weeks afterward.

Hélène moved into Jean's house. She embraced Kateri as her step-daughter, and over the years a close bond grew between them that was to last all their lives. Making a home for Jean and helping Tante Barbe at the inn filled Hélène's days, but she still had time for other people. La Soeur Bourgeoys bought a farm with a stone house in 1668, just for the *filles du roi* who would continue to journey to New France in the coming years. Hélène always visited the house when each new group of girls arrived, to offer welcoming words of encouragement and hope.

Hélène and Jean's first child, Marc, was born in 1669, to great joy. The husband of Marie who never speaks, Monsieur Lespérance, made the baby a fine cradle. A second baby, Catherine, came into the world in 1673. Born prematurely, she nearly died. Jean always thought that it was only Hélène's fierce love that kept the tiny baby alive. In time Catherine gained weight and thrived.

By 1679 Hélène's and Jean's family had grown to four: Marc, Catherine, Bernice (who was named for Jean's mother), and Louis (for Hélène's father). A larger home was clearly needed. Intendant Talon's patronage had assured Jean's success, and Jean could afford to purchase a bigger house on Rue Notre Dame. The family moved into this home that summer, and Séraphin settled into the rooms above the shop.

When she was sixteen, Kateri married a Mohawk warrior named Akonni, and lived with him at the mission of Kahnawake, not far from Montréal. There they raised a large family. On August 4, 1701, the thirty-nine Native nations signed the Great Peace of Montréal. The Mohawks, Akonni among them, arrived late, and so their chief did not make his mark on the document. It was done for them by an Onondagan chieftain. There would be peace between the French and their Native allies for many years.

Séraphin remained an assistant to Jean, but more and more he helped Tante Barbe, whose eyesight began to fail as she aged. He married a widow named Anne Charbonneau; they had no children, but took great pleasure in those of Kateri and Hélène.

Tante Barbe passed on peacefully in her sleep at the age of sixty-eight. She left the inn and her sizable estate to Hélène. Séraphin and Anne ran the inn for her. He eventually worked there as the innkeeper full time, since he was never able to acquire the skills necessary to become a master gunsmith. The inn stayed in the St. Onge family for many years, until it accidentally burned during the French and Indian War in 1759.

* * *

The journal of Hélène's father was finally published in 1682. To have the work done, Jean travelled to Cambridge, Massachusetts, where there was a printing press. Hélène treasured the leather-bound book and often read passages aloud from it for her children and Jean. The printed journal and the original are still in hands of Hélène's descendants, as are the diaries Hélène kept all her life.

Hélène's family was the centre of her world. Only books and writing came close in importance. She used some of her inheritance from Tante Barbe to purchase a few books each year from a dealer in

France. Slowly she filled their home with them, and even donated some to La Soeur Bourgeoys's school, where Marc and her other children all studied.

Jean Aubry died surrounded by his family in 1702. After a brief illness, Hélène followed him the next year. She was buried beside her husband in Montréal, her wedding ring on her finger. The wooden cross she wore all her life was left to her daughter Catherine. She wore it on her own wedding day, as her mother had done. The cross has been handed down to the eldest St. Onge daughter since that time.

The exact location of Hélène's and Jean's graves is unknown, but that does not mean that they have disappeared or that they have been forgotten. Through their many descendants, they and the other *filles du roi* live on today.

Historical Note

By 1663 it was clear to King Louis XIV, who was referred to as the Sun King, that his colony in New France was not growing quickly enough. There were few marriageable women; the population of New France was largely male. The men could have married Native women, but they did not, even though for a time they were encouraged to do so by the Catholic church. Only seven marriages between Natives and non-Natives were recorded at Montréal between 1642 and 1712.

Respectable women had to be brought from France, then. The King, who considered all the inhabitants of New France to be his "children," agreed that the young women would be provided for with money from his royal treasury. Their travelling expenses would be paid, and they would receive a dowry of goods, as was typical for country girls. These young women were what we now refer to as *les filles du roi*. The term was not actually used until after 1667; it was first seen in Marguerite Bourgeoys's memoirs. The girls were simply called *les filles à marier*, or marriageable girls.

In 1663 the first *filles à marier* sailed to New

France. By the time Intendant Jean Talon arrived in 1665, the program was well underway. The names of more than seven hundred of the *filles du roi* have been documented. In the beginning most of them were orphans from the cities; some were of minor nobility. But it was soon discovered that country girls tended to deal better with the harsh life of heavy work and severe winters that faced them.

It was a daunting and perilous adventure. *Filles du roi* left France from either Dieppe or La Rochelle. Crossing the Atlantic in a seventeenth-century sailing vessel was no small thing. Conditions were extremely cramped and uncomfortable. In bad weather the ship would be sealed up, the food was dreadful, and some of the *filles du roi* were badly treated. There are cases of their clothing being stolen. At least sixty of them died at sea during the years the *filles du roi* sailed over.

Once they arrived in New France, the first stop for the *filles du roi* was at the town of Québec. Then, if they had not married, they would leave for Montréal or Trois-Rivières. Well chaperoned, they stayed under the supervision of respectable women such as Marguerite Bourgeoys until they agreed to wed. Some of the marriages were very hurried, businesslike affairs, but other *filles du roi* waited as long as a year before they accepted proposals. Robust, healthy young women were preferred, since they

195

would more easily adapt to hard work. Once a couple had come to an agreement, a marriage contract was first drawn up by a notary, in which the couple's goods were listed. A wedding would follow. Most of the couples wed in the fall, since the ships had arrived by then and the crops were in. Some of the marriage contracts tell about more money being given to the *filles du roi* by the King.

Existence was unbelievably difficult for the habitants. The work was hard. Their food was simple and sometimes not the best, with coarse bread being the centre of people's diets. Some habitants' homes were very primitive and their possessions few. To have a single change of clothing and a few sticks of furniture was not uncommon.

Medicine was in its infancy and the illnesses that we can easily deal with today were devastating. People had no idea what caused scurvy. It was a common ailment both during the ships' crossings, and in the winters of New France when fresh food was unavailable. The cabbage soup that Hélène and Tante Barbe brought to the sick men would have contained the vitamin C necessary to help combat it. Spruce beer also contains vitamin C. (When Jacques Cartier was on his third voyage in New France during the winter of 1536, most of his men developed scurvy. Many died. The lives of those who suffered from the disease were saved by the drink that the Natives showed them how to prepare with cedar twigs and greenery.)

Smallpox ravaged settlements of New France and the Native villages many times. There was a particularly terrible epidemic in 1687. Smallpox was yet another misunderstood sickness, and Hélène would have had no real idea of why she did not catch it from her father or from Jean. Both she and Kateri would have been immune — that immunity having come from the fact that they had each had cowpox.

The lavender and cedar smoke that Hélène used to fumigate the house was more than a folk remedy. It would have been effective with some illnesses, particularly plague, since the smoke would have killed the fleas that carried the disease.

The Natives who lived in New France were a constant threat to the settlers who had moved onto lands that had once been theirs. At times the habitants could not even leave Montréal to tend their fields. Travel was dangerous — travellers might be killed or taken prisoner. Finally, the Carignan-Salières Regiment was sent from France in 1665 to protect the settlements. Native villages were burned and it became clear to the Mohawks that there was only one course of action left to them. By July 10, 1667, the Mohawks agreed to peace, and the Regiment was sent home. Lured by the prospects of land, however, many of the soldiers remained in New

France and wed *filles du roi*.

In spite of these hardships, almost all of the *filles du roi* married, since it was a great disgrace for them not to do so. Some of the men, however, clearly would have preferred to remain bachelors, and the arrival of the *filles du roi* was not celebrated by everyone. But pressure was brought upon the reluctant bridegrooms. In 1670 Intendant Jean Talon decreed that unless a man married one of the *filles du roi* within fifteen days of the arrival of a ship from France, he would lose his right to trade and hunt. It was a fine plan, but one that proved to be extremely difficult to enforce.

In 1665 Jean Talon carried out the first census of New France. The population was more than 3000. By 1673, when the *filles du roi* program ended, the non-Native population of New France had risen to 6700. It was clear that bringing the *filles du roi* to New France had been an excellent plan.

The young women who bravely faced such an unknown future did so for many reasons. Some chose willingly. Others were driven by desperation. Each of their stories is different, but all have left the same remarkable legacy: the descendants who now may be found in many different places in the world. New France and its success owed a great debt to these courageous, hard-working women. So does all of Canada.

Jacques Cartier's ships arriving at Stadacona (later called Québec) on the St. Lawrence River, in 1535.

Samuel de Champlain's arrival at Québec, with canoes surrounding his ship. Champlain made a number of voyages to New France.

A monument to Paul de Maisonneuve, who brought some of the first settlers to New France and founded a mission community at Ville-Marie, later called Montréal.

Jean Talon, Intendant of New France.

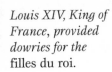

Louis XIV, King of France, provided dowries for the filles du roi.

A representation of Québec City in 1699, with the settlement on the hill, ships on the St. Lawrence River, and indigenous people in the foreground.

Jean Talon visiting settlers in their home.

Soeur Marguerite Bourgeoys, a teacher, came to Ville-Marie in 1653, and set up a school in a stable given to her by Paul de Maisonneuve. She acted as chaperone to the filles du roi *who arrived from France.*

The stone stable donated to Margeurite Bourgeoys by de Maisonneuve on November 25, 1657. Montréal's first school was officially opened on April 30, 1658.

Jeanne Mance was one of the first women to arrive in New France with Paul de Maisonneuve. She established Hôtel-Dieu hospital in Montréal and spent more than thirty years at work there.

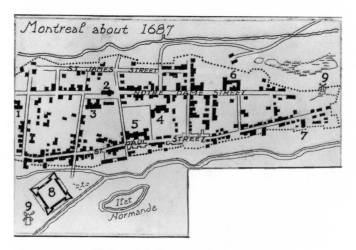

A street map of Montréal about 1687, showing the various streets and buildings.

A rather romantic version of Les Filles du Roi, *dressed in their finery, arriving in Québec.*

A farmer or habitant, wearing snowshoes and carrying a musket.

A depiction of part of a palisaded Huron-Iroquois village.

An Iroquois. The term sauvage *was often applied by the European settlers to non-Catholics.*

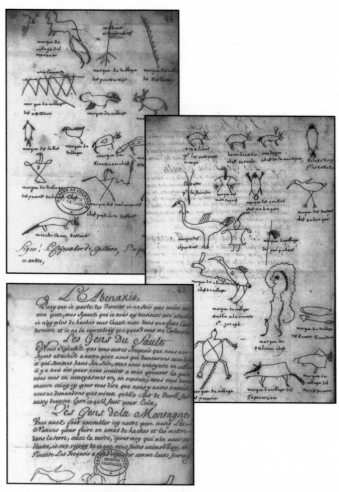

Part of the Great Peace of Montreal, signed in 1701, with totems given as signatures by the chiefs. For a time, the Great Peace brought to an end the conflict between the French and the Natives in New France.

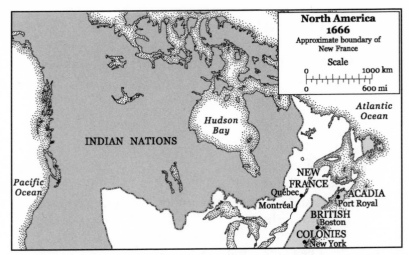

Although France claimed the territory shown above, actual European settlement stretched little farther west than Montreal, pressed on all sides by Native populations.

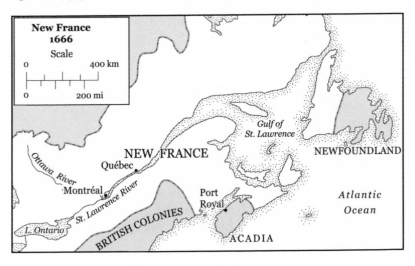

Glossary of French Words

arpent: about a third of a hectare or eight-tenths of an acre

bottes sauvages: winter shoes made of heavy greased leather

brun: brown

capote: a heavy coat

c'est dommage: too bad

chausson: slipper

chemise: a garment worn under the *corps*, bodice, and skirt; a shift

chignon: a "bun," a common hairstyle

coiffe: a head covering of light cloth

Compagnie des Indes Occidentales: the Company of the West Indies

corps: stays, a close-fitting undergarment stiffened with bone or wood strips, worn tightly laced

courge: gourd

denier: a copper coin worth little

écu: a silver coin worth six *livres*

écuelle: a two-handled pottery bowl

engagé: a hired man whose contract ran for 3 years

faux pas: mistake

fête: a celebration

habitant: one who owns land

Le Chat Blanc: The White Cat

livre: seventeenth-century unit of money; there was no *livre* coin, but 1 *livre* equaled 20 *sols*

lucet: a lyre-shaped tool used for making square cord

mocassin: French spelling for the English word, *moccasin*

noisette: hazelnut

ourson: little bear

potage: soup

Sainte Vierge: the Virgin Mary

les sauvages: a term the French used with regard to the Native population, meaning non-Catholic

sol: a copper coin worth 12 *deniers*

toise: a measure of about 1.9 metres or about 6 feet

tourtière: meat pie

tric-trac: a game something like backgammon

Glossary of Mohawk Words

enniska: February, lateness

kanon'tinekens: milkweed

Kateri: Catherine

kwe: hello

oniehte: snow

onen: good-bye

orye: friend

Teh hon tsi kwaks eks: lacrosse

wakatshennonni: I am happy.

A 1658 Recipe for
Potage of Herbs

Warm some water with butter and salt then take sorrell, buglos, burredge, succory, or lettice and beets.

After they are well cleansed, cut them, and put them in an earthen pot with the first cut of a loaf.

Boile all some while until it be well consumed, then stove your bread, take up and serve.

This recipe was translated or, as they wrote at that time, "Englished," in 1658. Sorrell refers to the leaves of wood sorrel. Bugloss (also called borage) is a coarse, hairy herb. Succory is chicory, a plant that was used for salads. Note the seventeenth-century spelling of the various ingredients, including lettice *for* lettuce. To stove *means to soak.* Well consumed *means* fully cooked.

Acknowledgments

Grateful acknowledgment is made for permission to reprint the following:

Cover portrait: Detail from *The Knitting Girl (La Tricoteuse)*, by William Adolphe Bougeureau, courtesy of Joslyn Art Museum, Omaha, Nebraska JAM.1931.106

Cover background: Detail from *Arrival of Jacques Cartier at Stadacona, 1535, Quebec*, by Walter Baker, National Archives of Canada C-011510

Page 199 (upper): Walter Baker, *Arrival of Jacques Cartier at Stadacona, 1535, Quebec,* National Archives of Canada C-011510

Page 199 (lower): George Agnew Reid, *Arrival of Champlain at Québec*, National Archives of Canada C-011015

Page 200 (upper): Statue to Paul de Maisonneuve, National Archives of Canada C-69552

Page 200 (centre): Jean Talon, Intendant of New France, National Archives of Canada C-69553

Page 200 (lower): Edmond Lechevallier-Chevignard, *Louis XIVth as a young man*, National Archives of Canada C-017650

Page 201 (upper): Jean-Baptiste-Louis Franquelin, *Veue de Quebec* [1699], National Archives of Canada C-015791

Page 201 (lower): Lawrence R. Batchelor, *Jean Talon Visiting Settlers*, National Archives of Canada C-011925

Page 202 (upper): Henri Beau, *Margeurite Bourgeois Fondatrice 1653*, National Archives of Canada C-012340

Page 202 (lower): The stone stable donated to Margeurite Bourgeoys by Maisonneuve, Nov. 25, 1657, National Archives of Canada C-012340

Page 203 (upper): Jeanne Mance, National Archives of Canada C-14360

Page 203 (lower): Charles William Jefferys, Map of Montreal About 1687, National Archives of Canada C-69551

Page 204 (upper): Eleanor Fortescue Brickdale, *Les Filles du Roi, Quebec*, National Archives of Canada C-201206

Page 204 (lower): Henri Beau, *Un colon de la baie d'Hudson du 17me Siècle*, National Archives of Canada C-1020

Page 205 (upper): Charles William Jefferys, *Part of a Palisaded Huron-Iroquois Village*, National Archives of Canada C-69767

Page 205 (lower): J. Laroque Sculp, *Sauvage Iroquois*, National Archives of Canada C-3164

Page 206: The Great Peace of Montreal, National Archives of Canada C-147864, C-147865, C-147866

Page 210 : Recipe for Potage from *The French Cook,* François Pierre La Varenne. "Englished" by L.D.G., 1658.

Page 207: Maps by Paul Heersink/Paperglyphs. Map data © 2002 Government of Canada with permission from Natural Resources Canada.

Thanks to Barbara Hehner for her careful checking of the manuscript; and to Andrew Gallup, historian, writer and editor of the journal, *Interprétant Nouvelle France*.

For Lauren Jones,
my niece in the 18th century

About the Author

While researching *Alone in an Untamed Land*, author Maxine Trottier made some discoveries she hadn't anticipated. Though she has known for years that her mother's family has been in Canada since the seventeenth century — it is a source of family pride — she did not know that the wife of one of her ancestors was actually a *fille du roi*. That revelation was fascinating enough, but an even bigger one was in store. It is almost as if Maxine were fated to write the story of Hélène St. Onge. Here is the "trail" that led her to write this book.

"In 1681, a census was taken in Montréal. Among the population was listed a twenty-eight-year-old tailor named Pierre Chesne dit St. Onge, who came to New France from the village of Reignac, in the province of Saint-Onge. He was my ancestor. There is no record of when Pierre actually arrived in New France; in fact, there are only two complete ships' passenger lists available.

"Pierre married Louise-Jeanne Bailly on November 29, 1676, in Montréal. He was contracted to work 'out west' from May of 1686 until May of 1695, which means he was a coureur de bois, not unlike the men in this story. I can only imagine the effect this might have had upon their marriage. Pierre and Louise-Jeanne did, however, have seven children. One of these was their son Pierre, born in 1698, from whom I am descended.

"Louise-Jeanne died on June 29, 1699. Pierre took a second wife on October 9, 1700, a woman named Marie Moitié. She did not figure largely in our family history, since none of us is descended from her. However, as I did the research for this book, it became clear that family ties and the course of this story were closer than I had ever dreamed.

"Marie had been a widow. Her first husband had been Jean Magnan dit Lespérance, a soldier in the Carignan-Salières Regiment. Marie's occupation is listed as having been a *cabaretière* — she kept a hotel and restaurant. This she did with her husband until his death in 1693. Until she married Pierre, she alone had been the proprietor of the establishment. Even more remarkable than all those details is the fact that Marie Moitié, who would have been my step-grandmother all those years ago, was a *fille du roi*. I decided to base the character of Tante Barbe on this woman, and to use other family names as well. I have set Tante Barbe's house on the street where it was actually located."

This coincidence, amazing in itself, set the stage for a later discovery. Maxine herself is directly descended from another *fille du roi*, a woman named Catharine Ducharme. Catherine arrived in Canada in 1671, at about the age of fourteen. She married Pierre Roy dit Saint-Lambert the next year. One of their sons, Pierre Roy, married Marguerite Ouabankikove, a woman of the Miami tribe and the sister of chief Le Pied Froid, at Fort Detroit in 1703. Maxine is their descendent. How interesting that she had decided that Hélène's older sister would be named Catherine, long before she knew of her *fille du roi* ancestor.

A former teacher and an avid sailor, Maxine has long been fascinated by history. She is a historical re-enactor, and part of a unit called *Le Detachement*, whose members portray the habitants of eighteenth-century New France. Now she is also an associate member of *La Société des Filles du roi et soldats du Carignan*, whose purpose is "to honour the memory of these courageous people."

Maxine is the award-winning writer of numerous books for young people, including *Claire's Gift* (winner of the Mr. Christie's Book Award); *Laura: A Childhood Tale of Laura Secord*; the *Circle of Silver Chronicles* (whose initial book won the CLA Book of the Year Award); and *The Tiny Kite of Eddie Wing* (winner of the CLA Book of the Year Award).

National Library of Canada Cataloguing in Publication

Trottier, Maxine
Alone in an untamed land : the diary of Héléne St. Onge /
Maxine Trottier.

(Dear Canada)
ISBN 0-439-98969-8

I. Title. II. Series.

PS8589.R685A75 2003   jC813'.54   C2002-904296-8
                          PZ7

6 5 4 3 2 1   Printed in Canada   03 04 05 06 07

The display type was set in Dorchester.
The text was set in Esprit Book.

✤

Printed in Canada
First printing January 2003

✤

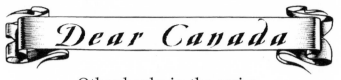
Dear Canada

Other books in the series:

A Prairie as Wide as the Sea
The Immigrant Diary of Ivy Weatherall
by Sarah Ellis

Orphan at My Door
The Home Child Diary of Victoria Cope
by Jean Little

With Nothing but Our Courage
The Loyalist Diary of Mary MacDonald
by Karleen Bradford

Footsteps in the Snow
The Red River Diary of Isobel Scott
by Carol Matas

A Ribbon of Shining Steel
The Railway Diary of Kate Cameron
by Julie Lawson

Whispers of War
The War of 1812 Diary of Susanna Merritt
by Kit Pearson